OVER DRIVE

ARIEL TACHNA

Dreamspinner Press

Published by
Dreamspinner Press
4760 Preston Road
Suite 244-149
Frisco, TX 75034
http://www.dreamspinnerpress.com/

Cover Art by Justin James   dare.empire@gmail.com
Cover Design by Mara McKennen

ISBN: 978-1-61581-902-7

Printed in the United States of America
First Edition
April 2011

eBook edition available
eBook ISBN: 978-1-61581-903-4

To Ryu,
who introduced me
to the world of racing
and made sure I got
the details right.

CHAPTER ONE

"PUTAIN de merde, qu'est-ce vous faites? Vous ne pouvez pas lire les indications que vous avez écrites vous-même?"

Daniel Leroux glared at his co-driver in frustration as they finally came to a stop. He'd lost count of how many times the car flipped this time, but this was not the first time his co-driver's errors had led to them rolling and being eliminated from a race. He could just see his rank falling as once again a rally ended with no points in his score column.

The crowd rushed over to make sure they were unhurt. Daniel summoned a smile as he pulled himself from the car to the cheers of the fans. Finland was a hard course, and he wasn't the first driver to wipe out on this turn, nor would he be the last, he was sure, but his co-driver telling him the road curved left instead of right was more than a miscalculation. It was the kind of gross error that got people killed. He didn't plan on being one of them. When they got back to the hotel where they were staying for the week, Daniel intended to talk to the team manager. He was already out of contention for this season. Even if they won every remaining rally, they couldn't catch the leader, and they'd have to come in third or above in every remaining race to end up in the top five. With a co-driver he could trust, he might have done it. With the idiot climbing out of the car on the other side as co-driver, he'd be lucky to be alive still at the end of the season.

The spectators helped push the car back onto the road, allowing Daniel to continue down the course, but he didn't push the time. He could hear from the sounds coming from the engine that they wouldn't make it at high speeds. He'd get off the course so it was clear for the next driver and then withdraw from the rest of the race.

"I'M SORRY, Jean-Paul," Daniel said, tossing his helmet and gloves on the table as he turned to face the team manager. "I can't work with him anymore. I've tried and tried. Watch the onboard if you don't believe me. A little off with the timing is bad enough, but telling me it would be a left turn instead of a right turn is more than bad timing. We're lucky we weren't killed."

"You mean we're lucky you're a damn good driver," Jean-Paul corrected. "Even with Isabelle working her magic, it's going to take time to repair the car. So what are you thinking, Dany, besides that you want me to fire Xavier?"

"I'm thinking that we can't even pull off a respectable place this year," Daniel replied. "I think we should withdraw from the remaining races and spend the rest of the year and the off-season training up a new co-driver, someone I can really work with this time."

"Did you have somebody in mind?" Jean-Paul asked. "Or should I look at the draft and see who's available?"

"There was a kid who was co-driving in the J-WRC," Daniel said. "A Canadian. Frank something. His career seemed to be taking off and then his team let him go. I liked what I saw of him before that. And he was with a French-speaking team, so he's got to be at least conversational in French, which is good, since I doubt I could follow pace notes in English. Can you find out what happened and see if he's available?"

Jean-Paul's eyebrows lifted. "You've been thinking about this, haven't you?"

"Yeah," Daniel admitted. "I kept hoping we could make it through this season with a decent showing, but it isn't going to happen, so I'd rather make the break now and come back strong for next year."

"I'll see what I can find out about your 'kid' and anyone else who might be available," Jean-Paul said. "Tell Isabelle so she can let the crew know we're packing up and heading back to Auvergne. We can spend the fall and winter there getting ready for next year. There are back roads there not even you have driven."

"You keep telling yourself that," Daniel said cockily, picking up his gear. "I'm going to talk to Isabelle and then get a shower." He stopped when he reached the door, turning back to face the man who had been in charge of his career for the last five years. "Thanks for believing in me, Jean-Paul. I know that what happens out there on the road is ultimately my responsibility, and I appreciate you not blaming me for the rough season we've had."

Jean-Paul smiled. "We expected this to be a shakedown year, with Christophe retiring last season and you having to find a new co-driver. We didn't expect it to be quite as challenging as it's been, but you've proven yourself. Second in the world last year, and by only a few points, is nothing to throw away. We'll have more time to find a good match since we're starting early now. Don't worry. We'll get this team back on track."

Daniel summoned a smile in return, but it faded when the door closed behind him. Number two in the world last year, and not even ranked this year because he didn't finish the season. Talk about a bitter pill to swallow. Jean-Paul could say what he wanted. Daniel knew he'd let a lot of people down with his record this year. He'd be okay because he brought in more money in a year, even an off year, than he could reasonably spend, but he had no idea what would happen to the mechanics on the team once they were all back in Auvergne and the car was ready to go. Isabelle could handle the maintenance on the training runs since they wouldn't have the tight schedule of a rally. Unless he busted up completely like he'd done today, most of the mechanics would be sent home for the off-season. Usually, that was a matter of a month or two between the last rally in October or November and the first one in January or February, but it was only August now. Maybe he'd talk to Jean-Paul and see if something could be done for them. He wanted them to come back next year. Isabelle had talked several times about how well her team had worked together this year. If only he'd had as much luck with his team.

"Dany!"

He looked up and saw his sister and head mechanic rushing toward him. "*Salut, p'tite sœur*," he said, catching her in a tight hug. "I'm fine. I promise, I'm fine."

She glared up at him. "Did you let the EMTs look you over?"

"Isabelle, I'm fine," Daniel insisted. "No pain in my neck, no limping, nothing."

The fingers that dug into the muscle of his bicep were strong from working with cars all day and brooked absolutely no refusal. She marched him down the hall and out to the car. "If you won't show sense, I'll have to show it for you."

Daniel tried to resist, but he'd never yet managed to break free of her claws once she had a grip on him.

Three hours later, X-rayed and poked at until he was ready to snap, Daniel walked back into the hospital waiting room. "I told you I was fine," he said with a grin for his sister. "I'm always fine."

"You keep saying that, you might actually get someone to believe you," Isabelle retorted, punching the same spot on his arm where she'd dug her fingers in earlier.

"*Aïe*! Did you have to hit me right there?"

"Yes," Isabelle said with a grin. "Now come on. I want to know what you and Jean-Paul talked about for so long."

"Let's go back to the shop, and I'll tell you," Daniel promised. It would be easier to let his sister down there where she was surrounded by the cars she loved than it would be anywhere else. Damn, he hated this part.

Isabelle seemed to sense his mood because she dropped the sisterly hassling, driving to the shop in silence and parking outside the locked garage. She opened the side door and flipped on the lights, revealing what was left of the car he'd wrecked that afternoon as well as the spare car sitting beneath its tarp behind the first one. "I don't need to pull the tarp off and tune up the other car, do I?"

Daniel shook his head. "I'm sorry, *p'tite sœur*," he said. "We're going back to Auvergne as soon as we can get packed up here. Jean-Paul is going to fire Xavier if he hasn't already done it while I was at the hospital. We'll start looking for someone to replace him. Someone better this time. Someone who can actually help me win instead of making me lose."

"WHAT did you find out?" Daniel asked Jean-Paul when they met for lunch in Clermont-Ferrand, their home base, a week later. The bistro owner was a high school friend of Jean-Paul and always gave them a table in the back where they could talk in private.

"François Dufour, Frank to one and all, French Canadian, born in Montreal, bilingual, twenty-four years old. He drove with Ford's junior team for two seasons before leaving them at the end of last season. He didn't drive at all this season. Everyone was very closemouthed about why," Jean-Paul said, "which I found a bit odd. I did a little digging, and the official line was creative differences."

"That's bullshit," Daniel said. "They were winning. Not every race, but nobody wins every race. They were ranked second, and there had been talk of them moving up this year. I heard a rumor about a big new sponsor who would pay their WRC entry fees."

"The last two rallies they entered were disastrous, if you remember," Jean-Paul said. "I told you the official line was creative differences. I did a little more digging and found a rumor that he's gay. A rumor that surfaced right before the first bad race."

"You think they're related?" Daniel asked, his mind racing as he considered the implications, personal and professional, of having a gay co-driver.

Jean-Paul shrugged. "I don't know the driver of that team at all, except, as you said, that they were winning at the junior level. If he's homophobic enough to let it skew his performance on a course, that could be the source of the creative differences."

"In other words, their loss could well be our gain," Daniel declared. "It's not as if I care who Dufour sleeps with."

"No, you're just discreet enough to wait until we're away from a rally to hook up with men," Jean-Paul said.

"There are so many pretty, available girls throwing themselves at me when we're at a rally," Daniel replied with a cocky grin, "that I don't see any reason to turn them down. I like girls, too, you know." He sobered. It was one thing to make jokes about getting laid. It was another to gamble with his career. He knew his own opinion on the topic, but Jean-Paul had a lot more years in the sport than Daniel did. "Do you really think his being gay will be a problem? I mean, sure, there are the usual homophobic idiots, but thrashing them on the race course should take care of that. Our sponsors wouldn't want the blow of withdrawing their support because my co-driver is gay. The backlash from that could be significant. We aren't living in the Dark Ages anymore."

"No, I don't think it will be a problem," Jean-Paul said. "I wanted you to know what I'd found out, that's all." He paused and looked at Daniel with hard eyes. "I expect you not to make it a problem either."

"Me?" Daniel asked, trying to act innocent and failing miserably.

"Don't hit on him," Jean-Paul said bluntly. "He's off-limits for as long as he's your co-driver. Sex and cars don't mix. That's how people get killed."

"Fine," Daniel said, waving aside Jean-Paul's concerns. "I'll be good."

"Then we need to see if Dufour's interested in taking a trip to Auvergne."

JEAN-PAUL picked Dufour up at the train station and drove him out to the garage where they kept the cars when they weren't racing. Daniel held back, watching as Isabelle wiped her hands on a greasy rag and went out to meet them. He always enjoyed watching people's first reactions to his sister. On the rare occasions she bothered to fix her hair and put on makeup instead of pulling it into a tight knot to keep it off her neck, she was a stunner, but most men had no idea how to react to the more typical side of her: grimy jeans, old T-shirt, work boots, and grease-covered hands.

"So this is the new guy?" Isabelle asked Jean-Paul, hands on her hips above widespread feet. Daniel thought she looked as ready to throw a punch as greet the man.

"Frank, meet Isabelle Leroux, head mechanic for the team," Jean-Paul said. Daniel thought he could see Jean-Paul studying Dufour's reaction as well. "Isa, this is Frank Dufour."

To Dufour's credit, he didn't hesitate, offering his hand to Isabelle without even glancing at the grease. "Nice to meet you," he said. "From what I've read and seen at the rallies I've been to, you're a genius in the service parks."

Daniel raised his eyebrows in surprise. He had watched a lot of people on the rally circuit meet and dismiss Isabelle immediately simply because she was a woman. Either Dufour was a real charmer or he had done his homework. Isabelle *was* a genius in the service parks, but she didn't usually get much credit for it in the male-dominated sport.

The compliment and the offered hand had the desired effect. Daniel couldn't see Isabelle's face clearly, but he could tell from her stance that she was smiling as she shook Dufour's hand. "Do you need something to drink or a bite to eat before we head out to the course?" she asked, a courtesy she had never extended Xavier even after he was part of the team. "I have some Evian that's cold, and we can always send Dany into town for sandwiches. It's getting close to lunchtime."

"Monsieur Monier stopped so I could get something on our way out here," Dufour said with a nod toward Jean-Paul. "I'm ready to go as soon as everyone else is."

Isabelle's smile widened as she turned toward where Daniel stood, still hidden by the shadows inside the garage. "I'll get the car."

Deciding now was as good a time as any to show himself, Daniel stepped out into the heavy August sunlight. "Daniel Leroux," he said, offering his hand to Dufour. "Nice job with my sister."

Dufour shook Daniel's hand. "I'm not a fool. I may not have your experience with the sport, but I know the head mechanic is the most important person on a rally team. If the engine fails, the race is over."

Daniel chuckled. "And she'll never let you forget that. While she's pulling the car out, let me tell you what we have in mind, unless Jean-Paul filled you in on the way over?"

Dufour shook his head. "We talked about expectations in general, but not specifically about what you'd want me to do once we got here."

"There's a course out behind the garage. I know it well enough to drive it pretty fast even without pace notes, but with a competent co-driver and a good set of pace notes, I can cut a couple of minutes off my time when I'm alone," Daniel explained. "So Isabelle is going to take you through the course so you can make a set of pace notes. And then you and I are going to drive it together and see what the time looks like. Consider it a test rally. Only instead of racing against other drivers, we're racing against my best time."

"Do we have to beat it?" Dufour asked seriously.

Daniel snorted. "My best time was with a co-driver I'd worked with for four years who knew the course even better than I did. I don't know if we can beat it. Let's see what the results are, and we'll decide how it feels when we're done. It isn't just about the time. It's also about how it feels in the car when it's just the two of us. The kind of chemistry that wins races isn't something you can measure. You just know when it's right."

"Or when it's wrong," Dufour murmured, making Daniel think the other man had some experience with bad chemistry.

"Or when it's wrong," he agreed. "We just fired a co-driver because of bad chemistry and bad pace notes. There's Isabelle. Let's see what you can do."

Dufour nodded and walked over to the car, taking the helmet Isabelle held out to him and sliding into the car. Daniel walked around to the other side, leaning in the window before Isabelle put her own helmet on. "Don't try to scare him off. I like him."

Isabelle scowled back at him. "You just think he's cute." She pulled her helmet on and drove off before Daniel could reply.

Shaking his head, he moved to the fence behind the garage where he would be able to see a portion of the course. Isabelle wasn't wrong about Dufour, although cute wasn't the word Daniel would have chosen. Charismatic, maybe. Not quite handsome. His features were too irregular for that, but he definitely pushed Daniel's buttons in all the right ways with his sandy-brown hair, hazel eyes, and lopsided grin. Daniel couldn't tell exactly what kind of muscles were hidden beneath Dufour's clothing, but from what he could see, the Canadian had a tight, compact body, perfect for racing—and for fucking. He pushed that thought aside. Jean-Paul had been very clear. No messing around with his co-driver. It was too bad since Dufour was exactly the kind of man Daniel looked for in a bedmate. It remained to be seen if he was what Daniel was looking for as a co-driver.

CHAPTER TWO

DANIEL watched as much of the course as he could see from the fence line. Isabelle was driving relatively slowly, giving Dufour a chance to watch the special odometer installed on his side of the car and take notes about the distances and obstacles in the course. When it was Daniel's turn, they'd be driving three times that speed, perhaps even more on some sections. His stomach clenched in anticipation as the car entered the last leg of the course, making its way back toward him.

"Your turn," Isabelle said, levering herself out of the car and tossing Daniel the helmet.

"Can I have a couple of minutes to neaten up my notes?" Dufour asked. "I'd rather not make a mistake because I can't read my own handwriting."

"Take your time," Daniel offered. "There's a table in the garage if it'll be easier to do it there."

Dufour smiled and nodded, going into the garage in search of the table. "Well?" Daniel asked, turning to Isabelle. "What do you think so far?"

"He didn't blow me off," Isabelle began as Daniel had known she would. "He got right down to business instead of wasting time once he got here. He was on top of things in the car, asking questions about our standard of doing things, whether we used a one-to-six or a six-to-one scale on the bends, what speeds we considered safe for the different bends. We'll see how he does at two hundred kilometers an hour instead of seventy-five, but so far I like what I see."

"He wanted to make sure his notes were legible," Daniel added. "After all the problems we had with Xavier and misread notes, that's a real mark in his favor."

Isabelle nodded. "I know it's hard on this course, but don't anticipate. Try to base your decisions on what he says, not on what you know, so that it's closer to what it would be on an actual rally day."

It was good advice that Daniel was sure he'd never manage to follow. He'd been driving this course for six years. He'd try, though, because Isabelle was right when she said that on rally day, he wouldn't have the benefit of hundreds of times through a course. Even if it was a recycled stage from a previous year's rally, his memory wasn't that good.

Dufour came back out of the garage, pulling his helmet on as he walked, so Daniel did the same, taking Isabelle's seat in the car. "You ready for this?" he asked.

Dufour grinned. "It's been eight months since I've ridden in a rally car with a real driver, your sister notwithstanding. That's about seven months too long. I'm ready when you are."

Daniel checked the odometer and all the gauges out of long habit, despite knowing Isabelle had just been in the car. He trusted her implicitly, but he was driving now, which made it his responsibility. Pulling up to the starting line, he revved the engine a couple of times and waited for the signal from Jean-Paul. Through the microphone in his helmet, he heard Dufour's voice giving him the information on the first feature. "From Main Control 1, two hundred meters straight to square right."

Daniel knew it, of course, but he let the words run through his brain, creating his plan of attack as he waited for Jean-Paul to start the time. The moment his hand fell, Daniel's foot hit the accelerator, using the first two hundred meters to build up speed. The tires skidded as he took the first turn, Dufour's voice already talking him through the next one as he steadied the vehicle and prepared the next approach.

For the next ten minutes, he shut out everything but the sound of Dufour's voice in his ear and the car beneath his hands and feet. He didn't think about past drives or future rallies. He didn't think about the mountain on one side and the ravine on the other as they went through the more mountainous section of the course. He didn't think about Christophe or Xavier or Jean-Paul or Isabelle. He wasn't aware of the passage of time or the sweat rolling down his back in the August heat.

When they rounded the last turn and he floored it to cross the finish line, he let out a whoop of delight. Whatever the time, the drive had exhilarated him, leaving him feeling balanced again for the first time since the rollover in Finland. Spinning the car to a stop next to the garage, he pulled his helmet off, grinning at the man sitting next to him. "*Putain*, that felt good!"

Dufour grinned right back at him. "Hell yeah."

A moment later, Isabelle's excited face appeared in the passenger window. "Dany, that was incredible! You're only eight seconds off your fastest time ever."

Daniel's grin widened as he looked past her to Jean-Paul's smiling face for confirmation. "Ten twenty-four point one," Jean-Paul affirmed. "His record on the course is ten fifteen point seven."

"Then I think we need to talk business," Daniel said, getting out of the car and offering Dufour his hand.

IT TOOK a month to get all the paperwork processed so Frank could work in France and officially join the Citroën team. Daniel spent most of that time chomping at the bit. He finally had a co-driver he liked, and he wanted to start developing that chemistry. He understood that Frank was uprooting his life to come to France for most of the year and that the man needed to go home to get more than a couple of changes of clothes for his tryout, but Daniel wanted to get started. He had the simulator loaded with courses from all over the world, some from actual races, some randomly generated. Isabelle had both cars running at peak condition again. All that was missing was Frank.

He had spent the intervening weeks reacquainting himself with the area and with old friends and old pastimes. Jean-Paul scowled at him, and Isabelle glared, but Daniel ignored them both as he rediscovered the joys of rappelling and climbing in the gorges around Clermont-Ferrand. He hadn't found anyone to go hang gliding with yet, but he got a lead on a place that had ultralight planes. He had always wanted to learn to fly one, but he'd never had the chance. When Isabelle finally demanded to know what he was doing, he shrugged. "If

I can't drive, I've got to do something to get that thrill. I could try bungee jumping. Or maybe sky diving."

"You could try not getting yourself killed before Frank gets back and you can start training," Isabelle snapped, but Daniel just winked at her and went on his way.

Finally the morning of Frank's arrival dawned, the air crisp with the first hints of autumn. It would be another couple of weeks before the leaves started changing and falling, adding another challenge to their standard course. If they were dry, they weren't much of an issue, but if it rained, the wet leaves could make the curves treacherous. Daniel glared at the morning traffic on the road out to the airport outside of Paris, glad he didn't have to fight with that kind of congestion every day. As much as he loved coming to the capital for a weekend of anonymity, he never drove there for this very reason. Frank would have too much luggage to make him take the train, though.

He circled the airport a couple of times until his cell phone rang.

"*Âllo?*"

"*Bonne matinée*," Frank's voice said in his ear. Daniel rolled his eyes at the Canadian expression, but he didn't say anything about it. He'd wait until he knew Frank a little better before trying to break of him of his backwards expressions.

"Hello, Frank. How was your flight?"

"Long," Frank replied. "I'm outside terminal E."

"I'll be around as quickly as I can," Daniel replied. "It shouldn't be more than a couple of minutes."

Now that he knew Frank was waiting, Daniel drove with more determination, weaving in and out of traffic until he got around to Terminal E. He pulled over to the curb, hopping out to offer Frank his hand in greeting. Frank returned the handshake. "It's a lot warmer here than it is in Quebec."

Daniel grinned, thinking Frank looked good even when exhausted. The dark circles under his eyes weren't exactly attractive, but Daniel appreciated the tousled hair, like Frank had run his fingers through it repeatedly, and the scruff on his cheeks, the same sandy-brown color as his hair, sent images of beard burn through his mind. He coughed a little to hide his reaction. "Welcome to civilization rather than that wilderness you call home." He hefted one of Frank's huge suitcases into the trunk while Frank loaded the other one and his backpack and small suitcase. "Did you bring enough luggage?"

Frank rolled his eyes. "Do you know how expensive it is to ship stuff overseas? I carried everything I could because shipping the rest already cost me a month's salary."

"Send the bill to Jean-Paul," Daniel said as they climbed back in the car and Daniel followed the signs for the A1. "Your contract should cover relocation expenses."

"I didn't even think about that," Frank said with a shake of his head. "It wasn't an issue with my last job. It was close enough to home that I drove to the track during the week and stayed at the garage and then went home on weekends."

Daniel shook his head. "We'll do better than that here. My guest room isn't ideal, but it'll do until you can find a place of your own. Jean-Paul has a list of furnished apartments for rent as a start. You don't have to pick any of them, of course, but he thought that would speed up the process of getting you settled."

"You all are making this really easy," Frank said as they headed south. "I'm not used to it yet."

Daniel shrugged. "Here's the deal, Frank. I went from being in the top five with a co-driver who retired to being nowhere near that with a co-driver I couldn't trust. Our performance on the practice course was unbelievable. Jean-Paul is astute enough to know what that means for next season. If we can keep that and build on what we did when you were here before, we'll be on the podium more often than not, and that means money. Prize money, sponsorship money, merchandise money. Not to put it too bluntly, but you're the key to the cash cow here. We all want to be successful, and part of that is making you comfortable."

Frank smiled. "I didn't say I didn't appreciate it. It's a nice change, that's all."

Daniel laughed. "You're playing with the big boys now."

They spent the next hour discussing a schedule for training. They had the rest of September, all of October, November, and December, and most of January before the first rally. The next year's schedule hadn't been announced yet, but Daniel expected it to be Sweden or Finland, somewhere with plenty of ice and snow to add to the challenge of the course. The mountains of Auvergne would provide plenty of practice with that over the winter.

"Isabelle is a genius at mixing up the course we drove when you were here before," Daniel said. "She'll change it up on us periodically so we're actually driving instead of using the simulator all the time. Jean-Paul has been calling around as well to arrange some drives elsewhere in France, to get a good mix of tarmac and gravel, mountainous and flat. It'll give you a chance to see a little of the country while we're at it."

"I'm here to work, not sightsee," Frank insisted.

"We'll work," Daniel promised, "but we don't drive at night. We can enjoy some nightlife if nothing else. I know all the good spots."

"That's good," Frank said, but his voice lacked enthusiasm. Daniel almost assured the other man that he knew as many gay bars as straight ones, but Frank hadn't said anything, and Daniel didn't want to put him on the spot. There would be time for confessions later, when they knew each other a little better.

After about an hour, Frank started to yawn, the overnight flight catching up with him. "Take a nap," Daniel suggested. "We've got several more hours still and there's nothing all that interesting to see along the way. Not until we get off the highway onto the country roads. Then it gets fun."

Frank chuckled sleepily, the sound low and husky and very attractive. "Trust a rally driver to look forward to the part of the drive everyone else dreads."

Daniel grinned back. "There have to be some perks to the job."

Frank yawned again. "And all the beautiful women on your arm aren't enough?"

Daniel laughed. "They're definitely a side benefit. Get some sleep. Once we get home, Isabelle will want to start showing you the car and Jean-Paul will want you to sign papers and you won't have another chance to rest before tonight."

Frank stuffed his jacket under his head and closed his eyes, leaving Daniel alone with his thoughts as he drove. The chemistry was still there, fortunately. A part of him had worried that the drive they had done together was a fluke rather than a true indication of what their partnership would be like. Frank wasn't reading pace notes now, or even reading directions since Daniel knew where he was going, but the conversation had been easy, comfortable. The same kind of rapport he'd had with Christophe almost from the beginning and that he'd never developed with Xavier. They would build on that over the next five months as they refined their communication on the track and off, so that when Frank wrote the pace notes, he could accurately tell Daniel what to expect as he approached each section of a rally.

The attraction was still there, too, despite Daniel's better judgment. He knew next to nothing about Frank, certainly nothing about the man's private life. Hell, for all he knew, Frank could have a husband at home. He doubted it or it probably would have made the gossip rags at some point, but that didn't mean the other man didn't have a boyfriend.

Even if he didn't, it didn't mean Frank would return Daniel's interest. Or that he'd want to get involved with someone on the rally circuit, particularly his own partner. After all, Jean-Paul was right. Sex and cars didn't mix. There couldn't be anything but the race. It was one of the reasons Daniel's past lovers, male and female, hadn't stuck around. No one wanted to compete with his love affair with his car because they knew they'd never win. It was that single-mindedness that had gotten him to the top levels of the sport. He wasn't about to give that up for a passing fancy. He couldn't be distracted by a lover's spat while he was racing, or he and his co-driver could both end up in the hospital. Or dead.

Frank slept all the way past Orléans as Daniel turned southeast on the A71. By the time they neared Bourges, almost three hours into their trip, Daniel needed a break. Pulling into the rest area, he nudged Frank awake, the confusion in the other man's face endearing as he blinked owlishly, trying to wake up.

"*Quoi?*" Frank stuttered as his eyes opened, his Québecois accent far stronger than Daniel had ever heard it.

"*Quoi?*" Daniel mimicked. "It's time for a break. Do you want anything? Coffee? Lunch? There's an Autogrill here or we can go into town, although that will slow us down more."

"I always sound like my grandfather when I first wake up," Frank said defensively.

"It's charming," Daniel insisted. "It just surprised me because I'd never heard that strong an accent from you before."

"There are as many different variations of French in Canada as there are towns and regions where the language is spoken, even before you start mixing in English words with the bilingual population," Frank explained. "When I'm awake and aware of who I'm talking to, I use what would probably be considered the standard version, although I remember my sister teasing me about being a snob because I always spoke *pointu*."

"Pointed?" Daniel repeated. "How do you speak pointed?"

"With a crisp accent," Frank elaborated. "More like a Parisian and less like a Québecois. My grandfather had the really strong Québecois accent, the one that sounds almost like a duck quacking. I spent a lot of time with him when I was a child, and that accent still slips out sometimes when I'm not paying attention."

"So," Daniel said, changing the subject, "lunch? Coffee?"

"Lunch would be good."

They went inside the Autogrill, separating to make their own selections from the sizable buffet. When Daniel finished selecting and paying for his meal, he looked around for Frank, only to find the other man at the windows of the restaurant, looking out at the highway that passed beneath the restaurant. He crossed the room to Frank's side.

"This is really amazing," Frank said. "You don't see rest areas like this in Canada."

"The rest areas in France are second to none," Daniel agreed. "Come on. You need to eat so we can get back on the road."

Frank turned away and followed Daniel to a table. "How much longer?" he asked as he started to eat.

"About an hour and a half," Daniel said, digging into his own meal, "depending on traffic. It hasn't been bad since we left Paris, and we'll be in Clermont-Ferrand before rush hour, so we shouldn't have any problem."

"Will we make it out to the track today?"

"No one is expecting us," Daniel said. "Between the jet lag and the drive and wanting to let you settle in, Jean-Paul figured it would be tomorrow, if not the day after, before we'd be ready to start at the track. He might come by with papers for you to sign, but that should be it."

"Forget that," Frank said. "I can settle in later. I want to get started!"

Daniel grinned. "There's nothing to stop us from going by the track. If nothing else, we can drive the course in this car to talk it through together. It's not like you're going to unpack more than a few changes of clothes at my place anyway. Tomorrow morning we can look at apartments for you and tomorrow afternoon we can get the race car out and get started for real."

"I can't wait!"

"If you finish your lunch, we can get on the road again," Daniel teased.

They finished eating and headed back out, discussing strategy and analyzing the highway the way they would a course. It didn't present the challenges a rally would, but it let them look at bends and banking. When they neared Clermont-Ferrand, Daniel said, "We could take the back roads the rest of the way in. It will be slower, but a whole lot more interesting in terms of our discussion."

"As long as you aren't going to get us lost."

"No chance of that," Daniel assured him. "I grew up around here, but if I do get stuck, I've got GPS."

"What are we waiting for, then?"

Switching lanes to catch the next exit, Daniel let out an exuberant whoop as they left the highway for the two-lane country roads that wended their way through the Massif Central.

"Severity one or two?" Frank asked as they rounded the first bend.

"One," Daniel said. "Maximum speed, one hundred twenty if there are no obstacles or steep drops on either side. Note it if I can't use the shoulder as a buffer or if there's another bend on the other side so I'll slow down a little more."

"Hold on two seconds," Frank said, digging in his backpack and pulling out a notebook and pen. "If we're going to get into that level of detail, I'd rather write it down so I can go over it again later."

Impressed, Daniel paused his commentary while Frank got settled again. With Christophe, who had far more experience, Daniel had taken his cues from his co-driver. Xavier had never cared to go beyond the basics, never trying to push the limits. Frank seemed interested in really getting it right as a partnership, in establishing their own language that would let them communicate in shorthand with a precision that would let Daniel hit maximum speeds consistently.

"Okay, ready."

They spent the rest of the drive into Clermont-Ferrand discussing the roads, even turning around and backtracking a few times to ensure they agreed on a particular point.

"You use some different parameters than my last driver," Frank said as they reached the outskirts of the city.

"Is that a problem?" Daniel asked.

"Not at all," Frank assured him, "but it may take a few weeks to get used to the differences on a gut level."

"We've got a few months."

"It won't take me that long."

The confidence in Frank's voice was catching. "Do you still want to go by the garage tonight? We've gotten more done this afternoon out on the roads than we probably could have done even if we'd gone straight to the garage."

Frank shook his head. "A shower and a beer sound really good right about now."

"Shower at my place," Daniel said, "and then I'll take you to my café. They'll be thrilled to meet you."

"*Your* café?" Frank repeated.

"The one I always go to," Daniel explained. "You'll find yours too. Every Frenchman has his café. Where everyone knows everyone. The regulars, anyway. The place where I celebrate when I win and where everyone assures me it was someone else's fault when I lose."

"We're done losing," Frank insisted. "We may not win them all, but we're going for the championship next year. I can feel it already."

"Michaels will be the one to beat," Daniel said. "He's driving like a demon this year. He won in Finland, which almost always goes to a Nordic driver, and he's on course to win in Mexico now. I don't know what lit a fire under him, but something did. If he can keep it up, he could take the title this year."

"He drives better on gravel than he does on tarmac," Frank said. "I've been watching him too. If we can beat him consistently on the tarmac and sometimes on gravel, we'll have a chance at him."

"Then I guess it's a good thing I like tarmac better," Daniel said.

"We'll need to work on gravel, then," Frank insisted. "We have to be better than anyone on tarmac to stay in contention for the title."

Daniel nodded as he pulled up in front of his apartment. It was such a relief to be able to discuss strategy with his co-driver again. Isabelle was wonderful at it, but she wasn't in the car with him during a race.

"Let's get cleaned up. I'll buy you a beer for your first night in France and in town." He led Frank inside and pointed out the guest room and bathroom. "Welcome to the big leagues."

CHAPTER THREE

"ABOUT time you got here."

Isabelle's voice caught Frank off guard. "Daniel said he was going to tell you where I was this morning. I can't impose on his generosity forever. He'll want his own place back soon."

Isabelle scoffed at him. "He doesn't care. He just wants to race. Come inside. I'm working on the engine. You should help."

Frank followed her inside, perfectly willing to do whatever he could to help. If the car broke down during a rally, he'd have to fix it, and the longer it took, the farther behind they would fall in the race.

"The shell is a Citroën DS3 with a reinforced roll cage and a few other small modifications to the windows, since they want the shell to be mostly standard," Isabelle said as they walked into the cool interior of the garage out of the sun, "but the rest is anything but standard."

Frank had expected as much, but each team made their own adjustments within the guidelines of the WRC, and Frank would have to learn what magic Isabelle had worked on this one. Isabelle raised the hood and took Frank on a tour of the car. The engine, while souped-up by normal standards, was pretty typical from what he'd seen on rally cars. He nodded and followed along as she talked about improvements to the suspension and transmission. "But this is what makes the car really special. Dany hasn't even driven this one yet. I've just finished installing a paddle shifter. It will let Dany shift gears without ever taking his hands off the wheel."

"Is that legal?" Frank exclaimed, eyes wide. "I've never seen that before."

"It's legal," Isabelle assured him, "and we'll be one of only two or three cars using it. Once Dany gets used to it, it should cut seconds off his time."

And seconds were often the deciding factor in a race, as Frank well knew. "So when can we start testing it?"

Isabelle grinned. "As soon as my brother gets his lazy ass out to the garage."

"And you were hassling me about just getting here?" Frank asked indignantly.

"I don't like anyone," Isabelle retorted, her grin taking the sting from her words. "Haven't you figured that out already?"

Frank grinned back. "I think it's all for show. Underneath, you're a big softie."

"You'll never find anyone who'll believe it," Isabelle shot back.

"Not even Dany?"

"Especially not Dany," Isabelle said. "I've ridden his case since he first showed some talent for driving. He thinks I'm the world's biggest bitch, and I'd rather keep it that way if it's all the same to you. It keeps him listening to me."

"So come explain to me how this new contraption works," Frank said, peering inside the car. "If I'm going to have to fix it should it break, I need to know all about it."

"The regular gearshift is still in place and functional," Isabelle told him, going around to the other side and leaning in as well. "If the paddle shifter fails, Dany can simply switch, but I'm hoping to work all the bugs out of the system before the first rally next year so it won't fail."

They spent the next hour going over the specifics of the new system, Isabelle guiding Frank through all the technical aspects of the installation.

Finally, Isabelle stepped back, wiping her hands on a rag. "I haven't had lunch yet. Have you eaten?"

"I got something before I came out to the garage," Frank said, "but I wouldn't say no to something to drink."

"There's water or juice in the fridge," Isabelle offered, going to the sink and beginning the process of getting all the grease off her hands. "I love my job, but sometimes I could do without the mess."

"How did you get into the sport, anyway?" Frank asked, waiting his turn at the sink. "You don't exactly see a lot of women involved in the actual racing. They're usually show girls on the side. No offense."

"None taken," Isabelle said. "I can hardly deny the truth when it gets rubbed in my face every time we go to a rally." She dried her hands and stepped aside to make space for Frank. "My father loved cars and racing. He never made it as far as the WRC, not even on the junior levels, but Dany and I grew up surrounded by the sport. I think my father dreamed of us being the first brother-sister team in the WRC, but I can't handle the curves in the passenger seat."

"You could drive and let Dany be the co-driver," Frank said.

Isabelle shook her head. "Dany's the better driver. I might be able to compete at the J-WRC level, but I'd never win enough to get the sponsors to advance. Dany has a shot at the championship title. I'm not going to take that away from him—from us—for the pipedream of a man who died five years ago. Not when the title is a dream we can make come true."

"Whatever stories she's telling you, they're all lies."

Dany's voice—because Frank had already started to think of his driver as Dany rather than the more formal Daniel—jolted through Frank in an entirely inappropriate way. Fortunately, Isabelle replied to the insult in typical sibling fashion, giving Frank a chance to recover his composure before he rose to greet the other man. "All lies, eh? Then I guess you aren't happy I'm here and excited to get to work."

"I didn't say that," Isabelle squawked as Dany hurried to insist that he was very glad Frank was there. Dany's insistence did nothing to help Frank's equilibrium, but the interplay between the siblings made him smile.

"So what's on the schedule for this afternoon?" Frank asked more seriously when the squabbling stopped.

"Rolling out the new car," Isabelle said immediately.

"You mean you're finally going to let me see what you've been doing?" Dany asked.

"Only if you're nice to me," Isabelle said, winking at Frank behind Dany's back.

"I'm always nice to you," Dany said with a pout that made Frank want to grab hold of his lower lip and not let go. He excused himself with a vague noise about finding a restroom, needing a chance to pull himself together. He wasn't eighteen anymore, and he'd long since stopped thinking with his dick, but Dany shot his resolve all to hell. Five years ago, Daniel Leroux appeared on the WRC stage, paired with an experienced co-driver and racing like he owned the world. Frank was still driving local rallies at the time, but he had followed Dany's career from the start, dreaming in a fanboyish sort of way of having the chance to meet his idol someday. He had never expected that moment to come attached with a job offer. So far, he'd managed to keep it together, to act professionally, but he'd done more than follow Dany's career. More than once, Dany had featured in Frank's nighttime fantasies as far more than a rally driver, his black hair and sparkling green eyes and classical features enough to make him Frank's favorite imaginary lover.

Frank had promised himself not to let those fantasies interfere with his new situation. He had a chance at a future he had thought lost when his previous team let him go so suddenly and without recommendations. He couldn't afford to let unrealistic dreams screw that up, particularly when he had no reason to hope that Dany might be into men. Every indication in the media certainly suggested otherwise, showing photos of Dany with a different girl at practically every rally. Not that he actually thought Dany slept with every girl photographed on his arm, but Frank had never seen him photographed with any guy other than his co-drivers, his mechanics, and other drivers on the podium. Nothing to give Frank any encouragement at all. Now if only his body would listen.

Dany might not have given Frank any encouragement, but he also hadn't given Frank any discouragement. He'd driven to the airport himself rather than make Frank take the train or rent a car. He'd been fun and friendly and generous to a fault, giving Frank space in his apartment until Frank could find his own place. He'd been everything Frank had always imagined he would be when he dreamed of them working together, which made it harder to stop imagining him being something more.

"Frank? Isabelle won't let me in the new car without you."

Frank took a deep breath and ordered his mind off of his personal quagmire and onto business. "Coming," he called, stepping out of the restroom. He didn't give an explanation for his absence. Dany would assume he'd needed the facilities, and Frank saw no reason to disabuse him of that notion. "Let's go see what magic she's worked on the car."

Isabelle had the DS3 already out on the tarmac waiting for them. "Have you not seen what she's been working on?" Frank asked as they walked toward the car.

"Only from the outside," Dany replied. "She doesn't trust me under the hood, never mind that I learned as much from our father as she did, so I know it's a DS3 and I know she's made all the standard upgrades, but she keeps hinting at more."

Frank grinned. "Oh, there's more."

"She showed you already?" Frank nodded. "Isabelle! You're not supposed to share things with Frank before you share them with me. I'm your brother!"

"You're a pain in my ass," Isabelle retorted, "always trying to tinker with things that don't need adjusting. Frank already knows better than to do that."

Dany turned to glare at Frank. "No keeping secrets from me," he ordered, making Frank squirm a little at the thought of the big secret he was keeping. "If she tells you something about the car, you have to tell me immediately."

Frank glanced at Isabelle and back at Dany. "If she tells me something you need to know about the car, I promise to tell you immediately."

"There isn't anything about the car I don't need to know," Dany insisted.

"So if she tells me she washed it, you really need to know that?" Frank teased.

Dany hesitated for a moment, clearly considering the question. "Okay, fine. If she tells you something important about the car, you have to tell me immediately."

"Agreed," Frank replied, the lighthearted moment helping to ease some of the tension in his gut. He might not be able to keep Dany out of his dreams, but he could keep his dreams out of his workplace. "Let's take it for a spin and see what it can do."

The moment they climbed in the car and pulled their helmets on, Frank felt the lingering tension drain away. Here, in this environment, he had a job to do. "Do I need to read pace notes?"

"Not for this," Dany said. "I'm just going to drive around a bit and get a feel for the way it handles." He reached for the ignition, stopping when he noticed the unusual fixture installed around the steering wheel shaft. "Isa, what is this?"

Isabelle stuck her head in the window. "That, my dear brother, is what's going to make you win next year. You pull it and it will change gears without you having to reach for the gear shift. Hands on the wheel from start to finish."

Dany looked at her and back at the steering wheel, then back at her again. "*Putain de merde!*"

Isabelle's response was to punch Dany's shoulder. "Watch your mouth. You'll give Frank a bad opinion of you."

"Frank doesn't care if I curse," Dany said as he rubbed the smarting muscle with one hand, the other trailing over the paddle shifter with all the reverence of a man touching a lover. "So how does it work?"

"Pull the right side to shift up and the left side to shift down," Isabelle said. "Take it around the course once at a reasonable speed to get used to it. You can worry about times later. Right now I want you to focus on the new car, the paddle shifter, getting comfortable with it." Dany nodded, but Frank could see he wasn't really listening. Isabelle obviously could as well. "Frank, yell at him if he goes over one fifty. He doesn't know this car yet. None of us do. And I don't want him crashing it the first time he takes it out."

Dany spluttered in protest, but Isabelle reminded him sharply of the wreck that had ended the season three months early. That put an end to Dany's noise, but it served to remind Frank once again how critical his role would be. He'd watched the onboard video for that leg of the race, and the fault had clearly been with Dany's former co-driver. Frank didn't intend to make those kinds of mistakes. "Let's see what she can do," he said, bringing his own attention and Dany's back to the moment at hand.

Dany nodded and hit the accelerator firmly, but with perhaps less force than he would use at the start of a race. It was probably a good thing, since Frank caught him starting to reach for the gearshift between them on several occasions before he remembered the paddle shifter. Once, he hit the wrong side, downshifting instead of shifting up. It made for a jerky ride, but Frank simply held on and enjoyed being in the car with Dany. As Dany got more comfortable, Frank could feel his usual control returning, his speed picking up until he was nearing the one-fifty limit Isabelle had imposed. "Watch your speed," Frank warned. "Isabelle is very strict.

Dany's reply was to gun the engine on the straight, pushing the car well over one fifty and up toward one ninety. He let out a contagious whoop that Frank couldn't resist. Grinning, despite knowing Dany couldn't see him, he peered over the dashboard as best he could from his lowered seat and let the adrenaline rush through him.

Dany slowed as they reached the end of the straight, taking the car through a complicated series of twists and turns at a markedly lower speed than the first time Frank had driven the course with him, reassuring him that his driver could show sense when the situation warranted, even if he was a daredevil at other times. In his mind, he followed the course, making mental notes as he kept an eye on the odometer in front of him. Dany had said Isabelle would change up the course periodically, so this was more a practice exercise for him than anything he would be able to use later. With the differences in the way Dany noted certain bends compared to the way Frank's former driver had noted them, Frank figured he needed the practice so he wouldn't be responsible for any accidents.

Dany finished the course with a flourish, leaving Frank grinning and Isabelle scowling. "You don't do stupid shit like that on a shakedown run."

"Now who's cursing?" Dany retorted as he got out of the car, completely ignoring the content of her comment. It just made Frank grin wider. He could already tell working with these two would keep him on his toes. "The car drove great, *p'tite sœur*, just like I knew it would."

"And why did you know it would?"

"Because you worked on it," Dany said, pulling his helmet off and kissing Isabelle's cheek. "Any car you work on runs like a dream."

Isabelle huffed, but Frank thought she looked pleased beneath the scowl. He was surprised by how easily he could read her when Dany seemed completely oblivious to anything other than the face she showed the world. He'd keep watching, but he thought maybe Dany's reactions were as much of an act as Isabelle's. He pulled his own helmet off and smiled at her. "So how'd we do?"

"How'd you do what?" Isabelle asked.

"On the course, on the time," Frank said.

"I have no idea. I didn't time it since that idiot over there wasn't supposed to go over one fifty. I know he didn't listen to me, which means you didn't either."

"The car doesn't come equipped with a passenger-side brake," Frank said, although he had made little effort to convince Dany to slow down. "I can't slow him down if he decides not to listen to me."

Isabelle glared at him, but she could hardly argue. Instead, she stalked over to the car and drove it back into the garage.

"You've made her mad at me," Frank told Dany.

"She's mad at everyone all the time," Dany said with a shrug. "I've gotten used to it."

"How did the car feel?"

"It handles a little differently than the one I drove last season. It'll take some getting used to, but the paddle shifter is a real boon," Dany said. "I'll have to get used to it just like to everything else about the new car, but not having to take my hand off the wheel to shift will give me more control and speed things up."

"That's what Isabelle thinks too. Now we just have to get used to it, and to each other."

"We will. It'll just take a little bit of time. Did you see anything promising this morning?"

The sudden change of subject surprised Frank, but he switched gears mentally. "Maybe," he said, thinking of the apartments he'd visited with the agent Jean-Paul had contacted for him. "There were a couple that would be acceptable, although they aren't really my style."

"Yeah," Dany said with a nod, "that's always a problem when you're looking at furnished apartments. They fit some decorator's idea of what an apartment should look like, but that doesn't mean they fit yours. You can always put some of the things in storage and replace them with things you pick out."

"Or have my mother send a few things from Canada," Frank agreed. "The agent had a few other suggestions, but we ran out of time to visit them all. I have another appointment with her the day after tomorrow."

"Well, there's no rush," Dany said. "You're welcome to stay in my guest room until you find something that you're comfortable with. Don't sign a lease in a hurry just because you feel like you should."

"Thanks," Frank said, and he meant it, but he wasn't sure spending that many nights under Dany's roof was all that good an idea. Not when he already had problems controlling his imagination.

CHAPTER FOUR

"LET'S go kayaking tomorrow."

Frank looked up from the onions he was dicing to stare at Dany in surprise. "Kayaking?"

"Yes, kayaking. You know, a little boat on a river, with a paddle, and a guide, maybe, and nothing to do all day but shoot the rapids and have fun. It is Saturday."

"I know that," Frank said, "but I'd planned to spend the day searching for apartments since I haven't found one I like yet."

Dany snorted. "You can do that next week. I want to do something fun, and it's not nearly as much fun going by myself."

"You're like a little kid sometimes," Frank said, rolling his eyes. "All right. We'll go kayaking. Where are you taking me?"

"To the Allier valley," Dany replied. "It's nearby, and it has some incredible views that you can only see from the river because there aren't roads through a lot of that area. One of the few bits of true wilderness left in France."

"And the rapids?" Frank asked, returning to his task of helping Dany prepare dinner.

"Nothing too scary," Dany said. That answer did nothing to reassure Frank. Dany was an adrenaline junkie. "Nothing scary" was probably anything short of going over Niagara Falls. Frank had been to that waterfall and had seen the pictures of the daredevils who went over them in a barrel. Dany would fit right in.

"Give me numbers," Frank demanded.

"Level two and three rapids," Dany replied, tossing a pat of butter in the skillet. "Are those onions ready?"

Frank handed him the cutting board. "Okay, I can handle that. What do I need to do now?"

"Cut up the mushrooms while I sauté these," Dany said.

Frank dug in the refrigerator for the mushrooms, pulling off the stems and slicing them quickly. He handed them to Dany a moment later, inhaling deeply at the delicious aroma of onion and mushroom and butter. He'd eaten better since coming to France than he had in years.

"Now the pork cutlets," Dany ordered.

Frank grabbed them as well, unwrapping the white butcher paper so Dany could put them on the stove. Dany cooked the mixture up for several minutes while Frank set the table. He wasn't much of a cook, but he could get everything else ready while Dany did the real work.

"And it's ready."

Frank handed Dany the plates so he could serve the pork dish and the steamed green beans from the double boiler next to it. "*Bon appétit*."

The meal was delicious, simple but filling, the same kind of wonderful dishes Dany had prepared since Frank's first night in France. Frank had been diligent about looking for an apartment of his own, but he could admit to himself that part of his hesitation with each one was Dany's absence from it. He always found a more plausible reason to reject it: too far from a bus line, too small, too dark, too frou-frou. Beneath it all was the simple fact that he did not want to leave.

"So what else is there to do on the weekends?" Frank asked.

"Oh, lots of things," Dany replied between bites of his dinner. "Hiking, mountain biking, camping, rappelling, hang gliding. I even found a place that flies ultralight planes. And let me tell you what, ground skimming in an ultralight through the gorges around here is an amazing experience."

Frank laughed. "It sounds like you've already sampled that delight."

"Last month," Dany said. "The airstrip just opened, but it certainly won't be the last time. You should come with me next time."

"We'll see," Frank demurred, not entirely sure he could handle being flown in a small plane that way by someone else. In a rally car, he was perfectly content to navigate, but in pretty much any other situation, he needed to be the one in control.

"There's salad if you'd like some," Dany said when they finished their meal. "Or I can get out the cheese tray, although I haven't been to the store this week so I'm not sure how much is left."

"Salad is fine," Frank replied, shaking his head at how fresh everything was. Dany had gone to buy the bread that morning, and Frank was sure the pork hadn't been in the refrigerator yesterday evening, either. Dany didn't seem to think anything of it, just one more subtle difference between Frank's old life and his new one. He liked the new one.

Dany served up a lettuce and tomato salad with a Dijon mustard vinaigrette, again nothing fancy, but the mustard gave the dressing a bite that Frank very much enjoyed. "How did you learn to cook this way?"

Dany shrugged. "My mom died when I was ten, and Papa was always at the garage, usually with Isabelle. It was learn to cook or go hungry. Mémi, my grandmother, came to stay with us for a couple of months, and she taught me. Well, she tried to teach Isabelle, but I was the one who learned."

"I'm sorry about your mother," Frank said.

"She had ovarian cancer. By the time the doctors caught it, there was nothing they could do," Dany explained. "It was rough, but it was a long time ago."

"Doesn't make it any easier."

"No, it doesn't," Dany agreed, pushing back from the table and starting to clear the dishes.

Frank regretted the sudden loss of their easy companionship. Without thinking, he stood as well, putting a hand on Dany's shoulder. "I'm sorry I brought back bad memories. Let's go out to your café. Seeing everyone will cheer you up."

Dany summoned a smile, but it didn't reach his eyes. "Not tonight. We have to get up early if we're going to make the appointment with Canoë-France. We don't want to miss out."

The rejection stung, but Frank let it go. He had obviously hit a nerve with Dany, and insisting now would only make it worse. He helped finish the cleanup and went back to his room, flipping on the light and pulling out a magazine from his backpack. He flushed when he saw it was one of the racing magazines from early in Dany's career, proclaiming him the hottest thing on the circuit. Frank stuffed it back in his bag. He hadn't even realized it was in there. It must have been mixed in with his other magazines, because even without knowing he would be staying at Dany's place, he had decided not to bring anything that might give away his fanboy crush. The last thing he needed was for his new colleagues to discover it and have that create tension between them. His former driver had freaked badly just realizing Frank was gay. Realizing Frank was gay and obsessed with him would surely be too much for Dany. With a groan, Frank pulled out a different magazine and resolved to find a place of his own by the end of next week. As much as he wished he could just stay there with Dany, he couldn't take the risk.

THE wind was cool over the water as they pulled on lifejackets and helmets the next morning. The sky was light over their heads, but the deep gorges were still shadowed, adding to the chill as a light mist rose from the river. Frank almost wished he'd worn pants instead of shorts, but once the sun reached its zenith, he knew he'd be glad of the lighter garb. At the guide's direction, he stepped into the kayak, slipping his legs beneath the fiberglass panel to balance in the small boat. He had plenty of experience canoeing, but this was the first time he had ever gone out in a kayak, and the position was slightly awkward at first. Dany, on the other hand, was clearly an old pro, settling into the boat and paddling out into the placid stretch of water at the put-in point with an ease Frank envied. Somewhat awkwardly, since he had never used the double-ended paddle before, Frank followed until he neared Dany's kayak. "Don't run off and leave me," he said. "I don't know what I'm doing."

"It's easy," Dany assured him. "Just follow me when we get to the rapids since there's usually only one or two channels through them where you won't get stuck. Other than that, relax and paddle or drift with the current. This is supposed to be fun, not stressful."

That was easy for Dany to say. He knew what he was doing. Frank hated feeling like he couldn't control his body or the environment around him. The guide called for everyone to head downstream, so Frank applied the paddle, falling in line behind Dany and hoping he wouldn't regret the outing.

An hour later, he had completely changed his tune. Once he found the rhythm of using the double-sided paddle, Frank was able to relax and enjoy the fresh air, the bursts of spray on his face and arms, the warmth of the sun as it crested the walls of the gorge, and the thrill of shooting the rapids, even ones as relatively small as these. He wondered if there were other, more challenging rivers in the area, because he could see this becoming an addictive pastime, at least as long as the weather held.

Paddling close enough to Dany for them to talk, he called the question across the water.

"There are definitely harder rivers," Dany replied. "I didn't know your skill level, and even this one has its challenges, so I figured we'd start here and work up if you enjoyed it."

"I'm enjoying it," Frank said, his pulse pounding with the rush. "Maybe next weekend we can try a harder stretch?"

"Let's see how the week goes," Dany replied, "but if we don't need to be out at the track, then by all means, we'll up the ante."

They paused in their conversation to navigate the next series of rapids, the most complicated to date. Frank had to work to follow Dany, but he managed. "Damn, there's nothing like a good burst of adrenaline to get your blood flowing and your heart pounding," he said when they reached the calm at the foot of the rapids.

"I wondered whether you felt that way too," Dany said, returning Frank's grin. "During the week, I get it from racing, but I have to do something on the weekends, or I go stir crazy. It's just not enough to sit around and watch TV."

"So what are we doing tomorrow, then?" Frank asked. "We don't work on Sundays, do we?"

"Let's get through today first," Dany proposed. "We can see how we feel tonight and whether we want something physical like rappelling or hiking or if we'd rather something a little more sedentary like the ultralights."

Frank saw the wisdom in that since the kayaking used muscles not normally exercised by the work he did at the garage or by racing. He could feel his arms burning a little, not enough to slow him down, but enough that he would probably feel it in the morning. "Hiking or biking would be good, even if our upper bodies are tired. We aren't using our legs much."

"We'll have to see about finding a good bike for you, then," Dany replied. "The trails around here aren't anything to scoff at. I'm not sure I'd trust the average rent-a-bike on them, but we can hike until we find something I know won't give out on you halfway through a ride."

"Hiking is good," Frank agreed as they approached the next set of rapids, smaller this time. "Tell me how you know where the channel is."

"A lot of it is simply having been down this river enough times to remember," Dany replied, "but you want to look for rocks below the surface that could cause the kayak to hang up. We have a very shallow clearance, but even so, we don't actually float on top of the water, so it is possible to get caught by the rocks."

Frank studied the rapids ahead of them, trying to see a clear line through them the same way he would envision a race line on a complicated course. "I think I have it," he said after a few moments. "It looks to me like I can make it if I start far to the left and then cut sharply to the right about halfway through so I miss the rocks at the bottom of the chute."

"Good eye," Dany praised, making Frank glad he spent enough time outdoors that his tan would hide his blush at the praise. "Now see if you can do it without me ahead of you."

Hoping he wasn't about to make a fool of himself, Frank nodded and started toward the left side of the river, his eyes fixed on the point where he would have to turn sharply. The current picked up speed, taking him with it as he neared the spot. He managed the turn, but the rush of water at the base of the rapids threw off his balance and the kayak flipped. Fortunately, it righted immediately, but not without dunking him thoroughly. He grimaced as Dany navigated it behind him with ease. "So much for that," Frank grumbled.

"It happens to everyone," Dany assured him. "I can't count the number of times I've flipped. It just hasn't happened yet today. Besides, I bet you're cooler now."

Frank couldn't argue with that, the water taking away the heat and sweat of the day. "My shorts are going to get clammy."

"You'll just have to get wet again," Dany said. "We'll be to the portage point where we eat lunch in a bit anyway. You can dry off in the sun while we eat."

Frank stifled a groan at the thought of sitting around in wet, clinging shorts with Dany right next to him. That was so not a good idea, but there wasn't a thing he could do about it now except try to use his plate to hide any inappropriate reactions.

FRANK and Dany stumbled back into Dany's apartment an hour before dinner, both of them groaning about how much their arms hurt. Frank suspected Dany was playing up his pain so Frank wouldn't feel quite so bad about how much he ached, but he couldn't prove it and he wasn't about to challenge Dany over it. He kind of liked the idea that Dany would look out for his feelings that way. Even if it only meant they were becoming friends, it was still nice. Frank refused to hope it could mean anything more.

"Take a shower and let's go out," Dany said. "We can have a beer at my café and then go out to dinner. I want you to try *le tripou*. It's one local specialty I've never quite learned how to make, and I know a great restaurant where we can get some."

"What's in it?" Frank asked curiously.

"It's made with thinly sliced lamb, almost like pancetta, stuffed with veal or lamb and a mixture of spices. It's delicious, but it's way too complicated to make at home. You can get it premade, but I haven't found one I like as much as the fresh ones."

"It sounds interesting," Frank said.

"Have I steered you wrong yet?" Dany joked.

"No, you haven't," Frank had to admit. "All right, give me a few minutes to get the river water off and we'll go."

Dany grinned. "Great. I'll show you a different side of my city."

CHAPTER FIVE

"GODDAMN fucking piece of shit!" Daniel roared as he misjudged the same curve on the simulator program again and sent the car flipping through the verge. "What am I doing wrong?"

"You're missing the race line," Frank said. "You aren't cutting sharply enough in the first bend so you're in the wrong position to take the second bend at speed." He punched a button on the controls that superimposed a thin black line along the track. "Try it again. Slowly. Twenty kilometers, thirty tops, so you can see where the car is supposed to be at each point. Then we'll try it again at racing speeds."

"Why is this so hard?"

"It's supposed to be," Frank reminded him. "You're driving all the standard courses easily. These are the race breakers now, but instead of having only a few per race, this is obstacle after obstacle. You don't ever get a break."

"There aren't breaks during a race," Daniel insisted.

"Not coffee breaks, no," Frank agreed, "but there are easier sections mixed in with harder sections. This simulation is nothing but harder sections, the hardest sections. Drive the race line slowly so you get a feel for it. Then we'll try it again faster, and then we're taking a break. You're wound too tightly to relax into the rhythm of the race."

The problem, Daniel knew, was that it wasn't a race. As good as the simulators were, he needed the real feel of a car beneath his hands and seat, the real traction of the road under the wheels. He *felt* the road when he was driving in a way no simulator he'd ever seen could recreate. Unfortunately, they couldn't just drive around at racing speeds on the back roads of home or elsewhere without the expense of arranging to have roads closed for a period of time, and Jean-Paul would only pay for so many of those. They'd run the private course so many times that Daniel wasn't sure even Isabelle could come up with another way to change it, and while he was breaking his own records left and right there, it wasn't the same as a race. It needed to be January so they could get started.

Resetting the simulator, he followed Frank's advice, driving the race line exactly at a low speed. As he did, he realized where he was messing up. "Right here," he said. "I veered too far to the left right here and that messed up my entry into the next bend."

"Yes," Frank agreed, "so now that we see the problem, what do I need to tell you so that in a race, you don't have the same problem?"

"I think you're going to have to lie to me," Daniel said, "and tell me it's a sharper bend than it is because the bend on the other side changes the equation."

"So tell you severity four instead of severity three?" Frank verified. "That's going to slow you down more than necessary."

"Better to be a little slower and make it through the bends than end up on the shoulder or upside down," Daniel countered. "Even if we were able to continue the race, an accident like that is a much greater loss of time than taking the curve at s4 instead of s3."

"True," Frank replied. "Okay, let's try it again, at s4 speed this time, and see if that works better."

Daniel hit the reset button again, closing his mind to everything except the steering wheel in his hand and Frank's voice in his ear. Even though this was a simulation, they wore their racing helmets so Daniel would be used to hearing Frank's voice through the radio signal rather than directly. "From Main Control 1, one hundred meters straight to right bend, s4. Immediate left bend, s2."

Daniel made himself follow the directions, even though he knew the first bend wasn't a full level four. He hit the race line and made it through the reverse bend on the other side and out onto the one straight section of this simulation. "We did it!"

"Now we're going outside to ask Isabelle to create something like this for us and we're going to do it with the real car rather than a simulation," Frank declared.

Since that coincided with Daniel's fondest wish at the moment, he tore his helmet off and powered down the simulator. "What are we waiting for?"

They walked outside, only to be greeted by the first snow showers of the season, white flakes drifting softly down onto the gravel road. The snow had barely even accumulated enough to be visible, but it brought a smile to Daniel's face. "It's snowing!"

Frank chuckled. "You'd think I wouldn't be so excited every year given how much we get at home, but there's something... refreshing about the first snowfall."

"We probably don't get as much here as you do in Quebec," Daniel agreed, "but we get enough that I'm sick of it by the time winter's over if I'm here much. Of course, with the season starting in January next year instead of in February, we won't spend all of winter here anyway."

"No, we'll just spend it in Sweden racing on the icy gravel instead of here practicing on it."

"We should take advantage of the snow," Daniel said.

"How?" Frank asked.

"You talked about wanting to get Isa to set up a course like the one I had so much trouble with. Our first race is in Sweden, and it's now snowing. It seems like the perfect chance to tie all those things together into one practice run," Daniel explained, rubbing his hands together as he walked from the office where the simulator was toward the garage.

As he expected, Isabelle had the heater going inside the metal structure while she tinkered with the spare car, working on installing the paddle shifter on it as well.

"Hey, Isa," Daniel called as they shut the door behind them. "Can we drag you away for a bit?"

"Just don't waste my time," Isabelle called back, making Daniel roll his eyes.

"When do I ever waste your time?"

"Every time you open your mouth," she retorted. "What do you want?"

"We were hoping you could help us move around some of the obstacles on the course," Frank said, his tone much gentler than Daniel bothered to use. "We finally had a breakthrough on the simulator and wanted to see if we could carry it over to the track."

"Plus it's snowing," Daniel added, unable to keep his excitement out of his voice. "We can use the old car if you want so we don't mess up the new one."

"That defeats the purpose," Isabelle said. "You have to get used to the paddles in all conditions anyway so you may as well take it out. Just don't crash. I don't feel like fixing up another car."

"Don't be like that, Isa," Daniel cajoled. "You know I never crash on purpose."

"Idiot," Isabelle muttered under her breath. "What changes do we need to make to the course?"

Daniel might have been annoyed at Isabelle's change of tone when she spoke to Frank, but he didn't say anything. If Frank could get accomplished what they needed without having to spar with Isabelle, Daniel was happy to let him do it. It kept him from having to deal with her, if nothing else.

"Come on, *boulet*," Isabelle said when she and Frank started toward the door and Daniel didn't immediately follow. "I'm not doing this by myself."

Daniel trailed along behind the other two, looking up at the heavy clouds. He wondered how much snow they'd get. It was relatively early in the season, although snowfall in November was not unheard of. They didn't usually get any really heavy falls until December. One way or another, the tarmac was slicker than usual, even when it rained, as Daniel walked across it to the area Isabelle intended to move around in order to recreate the turns on the simulator. He'd have to be careful driving in these conditions or he wouldn't be able to keep his promise to his sister not to crash the new car.

He wouldn't worry about his time, he decided right then. He'd take the car through the course at road speeds first and see how it reacted to the snow. If it went well, he could always try a second time at a slightly higher speed.

"Are we ready?" he asked after he'd helped Frank and Isabelle move the barriers that constituted the edges of the course.

"Get the car," Isabelle said. "I'll tell you if you're ready after you've driven the course."

Daniel rolled his eyes as they walked back to the garage. They pulled the car out and drove up to the starting line.

"Okay, you know the drill," Frank's voice said in his ear. "From Main Control, one hundred meters then left bend, s4. Immediate right bend, s2."

"Got it," Daniel said, hitting the accelerator with less force than usual and easing the car out onto the track. The snow messed with his traction, reminding him to take it easy as he hit the first bend. He managed to follow the race line and hit the second bend at exactly the right place. His time wasn't great, he noticed when he pulled to a stop after he'd completed the bend, but he'd hit it dead center all the way through and he hadn't wrecked the car.

"I did it!" he exclaimed.

"Now do it again at twice the speed," Isabelle said, sticking her head through the window. "You didn't crash, but you aren't going to beat Michaels at that speed, even with it starting to get icy."

"Isa," Frank chided, "be nice. We just spent all morning wrecking simulation cars trying to get this right. It's a big deal that we got it at all. We'll work on the speed next. You just have to give us time."

"It's already November," Isabelle reminded them unnecessarily. "If you go home for the holidays, that just gives us a month before you leave and a couple of weeks when you get back before the first race. Time is something we don't have."

"That's still six weeks, or a little more since I was only planning on being gone a little over a week," Frank said soothingly. "You aren't going to help Dany if you make him so nervous that he can't concentrate. Go on back in the garage and finish the installation. I'll keep track of our times out here."

Isabelle humphed, but she did as Frank directed.

"Thanks," Daniel said. "She means well, but sometimes she works my last nerve."

Frank laughed. "That's what siblings do. My older sister's the same way, and I know I gave her hell, especially when we were younger."

"I keep thinking Isa and I will grow out of it," Daniel said as he drove the car back to the starting point. "We haven't gotten there yet."

"It's because you work together still and probably always have. You haven't had a chance to develop another way of interacting," Frank guessed. "My mom always used to say that things would get better between my sister and me once one of us moved out of the house, and she was right. I know you and Isa don't live together, but you're still in each other's pockets most of the time."

"Yeah, just about the only time she isn't on my case is when I go out to one of the bars in town," Daniel agreed. "She doesn't like the same places I do. She says mine are too loud and too smoky, and that the men don't want anything other than a body to fuck."

"I can see how that would annoy her," Frank said. "She definitely expects to be appreciated for more than her looks."

"Enough talking about my sister," Daniel said, staring back out at the track, calculating the way the road had felt beneath the tires and trying to figure out what speed he could take the curve at. "Let's try this again."

"From Main Control, one hundred meters then left bend, s4. Immediate right bend, s2."

The level tone of Frank's voice as he delivered the now-familiar pace notes settled Daniel's nerves, making him hope the effect would carry over once the racing season began. If he could relax into the driver's seat and not think about anything other than Frank's voice and the road in front of him, he might actually be able to win this season.

"LET'S go out tonight," Daniel said after they had finished working on the same bends several more times. "I feel like we made a breakthrough and we should celebrate."

Frank looked surprised at the suggestion, but he agreed right away, so Daniel let the surprise pass. "There's a great bar near your place," Daniel went on. Frank had found a place of his own within a couple of weeks of moving to France. Daniel understood the need, but he sometimes missed the company. "I could leave my car there, and we could walk to the bar and back. That way we don't have to worry about how much we drink."

"You're assuming I'll let you crash at my place tonight," Frank said, but his voice was warm.

"You'll let me," Daniel said confidently. "You don't want me driving after I've been drinking because you don't want anything to happen to me."

"You can crash at my place."

Daniel grinned. "I knew you'd say that. I need to go home and shower, but I'll meet you at your apartment at seven. We can eat at the bar. They have a pretty good brasserie as well."

"That's fine," Frank said. "I'll see you at my place at seven."

Daniel drove home as quickly as the now-icy roads would let him. He showered and took his time selecting something to wear. It had been a while since he'd gone out clubbing. Since Frank arrived, come to think of it. He hadn't felt the urge to go pick up random strangers because he'd been spending so much time with Frank, but while Frank definitely provided the company Daniel needed, he wasn't providing the physical release. Daniel knew why that was. He was sure Jean-Paul had given Frank the same lecture he'd given Daniel: *Sex and cars don't mix.*

It had been awhile, though, and Daniel was horny. He needed to get laid, and if he couldn't do it with Frank, he'd have to find someone else. The bar had a wide enough clientele that he could surely find someone to his taste.

Finished dressing, he looked at himself critically in the mirror. Black hair that just brushed the collar of his shirt, a hint of a five-o'clock shadow, green eyes that sparkled in the light, a fit body shown off by the tight line of his jeans and open-necked shirt. His dark running shoes completed the outfit, keeping his appearance casual enough for the bar without making it look like he was deliberately slumming. Yeah, somebody was getting laid tonight. Whistling cheerfully, he grabbed his coat and headed to Frank's apartment.

He almost completely forgot Jean-Paul's stricture when he got a good look at Frank as the other man opened the door. The tuneless happy whistle changed to one of appreciation at the sight of Frank's attire. He'd put on a tight sweater that outlined the muscles of his chest and a loose jacket on top of it. His jeans clung to his hips. His brown hair had the same tousled look of fingers running through it that Frank always had at the end of the day, except this time it looked intentional. "Looking good there, Frank," Daniel said with a grin. "Hoping to get lucky tonight?"

Frank shrugged. "It doesn't hurt to look good."

It didn't hurt at all, Daniel agreed silently. He only hoped he could keep his hands to himself. He wished he didn't have to, although he had no idea if Frank would be interested in return, but Jean-Paul's edict kept him from attempting to find out.

They walked down the cobblestone street of the old city to the bar Daniel wanted to visit. It was already busy without being overly crowded, allowing them to find a spot at the bar. Daniel greeted the bartender by name and ordered a glass of whiskey. Frank ordered a vodka and tonic.

"Not a hard drinker?" Daniel teased as he sipped his whiskey.

"Even if we're walking, one of us has to be sober enough to find the way home," Frank replied.

Daniel scowled at him. "I grew up in this town. I can always find my way home."

Frank didn't look convinced, but Daniel ignored him, tossing back his whiskey and calling to Nicolas, the bartender, for another.

"You're drinking hard tonight," Nicolas observed, but Daniel just shrugged.

"We're celebrating the first snow of the year," he said. "This is my new co-driver, Frank, by the way."

Nicolas offered his hand and Frank shook it. "He's obviously an improvement over the last one if you brought him out with you."

"Definitely an improvement," Daniel agreed, starting on his second glass of whiskey. "We'll have some wins next season for sure. It's time to put us back on the map."

"Glad to hear it."

Another customer drew Nicolas's attention, leaving Daniel and Frank alone. It didn't take long before one of the patrons of the bar sidled up to Daniel. He put his arm around her waist without even thinking about it, leaning down to whisper in her ear. She giggled, the sound suddenly grating on Daniel's nerves. He glanced at Frank, leaning on the bar beside him and thought, *What the hell? He's gay too. He isn't going to freak if I hook up with a guy instead of a girl.*

He loosened his hold on the girl, turning back to the bar as Nicolas came back to where they were standing. "Not interested in the girls tonight?" the bartender asked. "That's unusual. Or are you looking for more masculine company?"

Daniel laughed. "You know me too well. I won't rule anything out, but she was way too ditzy for me tonight. I'm not that drunk."

Nicolas laughed as well. "Plenty here to choose from. You want another glass?"

The moment Nicolas turned his back to get the bottle of whiskey, Frank grabbed Daniel's elbow.

"What?" Daniel asked, seeing the odd look on Frank's face.

"Why didn't you tell me you were gay?"

"I'm bi," Daniel replied automatically, "and it never came up."

"You knew I was gay," Frank insisted. "You should have told me so I wouldn't have spent so much time worrying it would be a problem."

"Did I really know?" Daniel challenged, because while he had, it wasn't really public knowledge the way Frank seemed to think it was. "You never told me."

"You had to know," Frank insisted. "Why do you think I lost my last job?"

"None of that came out," Daniel reminded him. "All any of us saw was a sudden drop in your driver's performance. They cited creative differences when you left, not your sexuality."

"And have a discrimination suit on their hands? They aren't that stupid."

"I know it felt like a huge deal to you—I know it *was* a huge deal to you—but the reason behind it didn't actually make the news," Daniel said. "Yes, I knew because Jean-Paul ferreted out the rumors, but I didn't see any reason to bring it up. It doesn't have any bearing on our professional relationship, any more than my sexuality does."

"You still should have told me," Frank said.

Daniel rolled his eyes and turned back to face the dance floor. He caught the eye of a blond near the far edge of the crowd who smiled invitingly. A part of him wished for something more than the random hookup, but since he wasn't going to risk his job by approaching Frank, he'd settle for finding some release elsewhere. "Enjoy your drink. I'm going to dance. There's a cute guy over there just begging for my attention, and I'm in the mood to give it to him."

CHAPTER
SIX

FRANK let out a long sigh as he watched Dany walk away. He couldn't quite decide how he felt about the revelations of the past few minutes. It relieved one piece of stress to know that Dany didn't have an issue with him being gay, but knowing that his driver shared his preferences, at least some of the time, and still preferred other company to his own was a bit of a slap in the face.

He supposed it ought to be a weight off his shoulders, knowing that Dany knew and didn't care about his sexuality. Certainly the fear of it coming out was gone now. The sense of betrayal at the reaction of David, his former driver, to the news that he was gay had been strong. They'd worked together for most of two seasons, had gone out together after races, and Frank had considered them friends. The shock when David refused to do more than drive with him in the remaining three races had been overwhelming. He had lost a friend, and he'd nearly lost his career.

"That's an awful sour look on your face," the bartender—Nicolas, Frank remembered after a moment—said. "Is the drink not to your taste?"

"No, the drink's fine," Frank replied quickly, not wanting the man to think he was unsatisfied. "I'm just a bit out of sorts."

"Dany abandoned you, I see," Nicolas said with a nod toward where Dany stood near the dance floor, clearly cruising the blond man who just as clearly had every intention of being caught. "There's plenty of other willing company around, if you're looking."

Frank shrugged. "Not really. I'm here to work."

"You've got to relax sometime," Nicolas said with a laugh. "What can it hurt?"

Frank didn't answer aloud, but he knew what it could hurt. If Dany took exception to anything he did and he lost this job, his career was effectively over. Co-drivers didn't have the visibility that drivers did, and if he was let go a second time, either because of his sexuality or because of his performance on the track, he wouldn't get a third chance. He had to make this work, and that meant not giving Dany any reason to send him packing.

He should have been over the moon to find out the object of his obsession played for the same team, or at least was willing to swing his way sometimes, but he couldn't do a damn thing about it. He couldn't take the risk of a misunderstanding between them affecting their jobs, because if it did, he'd be the one out the door.

With a sigh, he downed his drink and turned to the bartender for another. When he turned back, he caught sight of Dany disappearing through a doorway with his current arm candy. "Fuck," Frank muttered under his breath. He had no idea how he was supposed to stand here and watch the man he'd fantasized about for the last several years go off with another man, but he knew he wouldn't leave either. It was like watching a train wreck. You wanted to look away, but you couldn't. You had to keep watching until you knew what happened.

After half an hour, Frank had just about given up hope, wondering if there was another exit down the corridor instead of just the restrooms as he'd assumed. He was turning to pay his tab and take his leave when Dany reappeared at his side.

"I'm hungry. We haven't eaten yet," Dany said as if nothing had happened. "Nico, can we get a table?"

Frank stifled a groan. Dany seriously expected him to sit across the table and pretend Dany hadn't just gotten a blow job in the restroom? He chanced a glance at his driver and realized that yes, that was exactly what Dany expected. "Can I get another drink before we go?" he asked Nicolas. He had a feeling he'd need it.

DINNER was not as bad as Frank had feared. Dany laughed and chatted and completely ignored the elephant in the living room, talking about racing and training and everything they needed to accomplish before

Frank went home for Christmas. "With the snow starting to fall, I was thinking we should talk to Jean-Paul about getting a course set up way up in the mountains. It'll be expensive, but we need an unfamiliar run with conditions like we'll have in Sweden for the first race in January, and it's less expensive to set it up here than it would be to go elsewhere."

"That sounds reasonable to me," Frank replied, the safe topic making it easier to keep his voice steady as they talked. "I know you're familiar with the roads, but you can't have every bend memorized."

"No, I don't," Dany agreed. "And if you and Isabelle go with Jean-Paul to lay out the course, then all I'll have to go on will be your pace notes, and that will help too. Even if I know the roads, I won't know where you want me to go until you tell me."

"We won't have any time to judge it against," Frank warned.

"We won't have a time to judge against in a race either until the first person has driven it," Dany reminded him. "Simulators are better than nothing, but they can't replace actually being in the car on a course because no matter how good they are, they aren't an exact replica of the car we drive in a race."

Frank nodded. "We can call Jean-Paul in the morning and get him to set it up."

"In the afternoon," Dany corrected. "I'm not doing anything in the morning except sleeping." He pushed back from the table. "Come on. I want to dance."

Frank wasn't sure what that had to do with him, but he rose as well and followed Dany toward the crowd. Dany threw himself into the mass of writhing bodies with the same enthusiasm he did everything else. At least it wasn't about sex this time as far as Frank could tell. This seemed to be moving for the pure pleasure of matching the pulsing rhythm of the bass. Relaxing, Frank let his feet pick up the beat as well.

FRANK woke up at six the next morning, not even the alcohol and the late night enough to keep him asleep past his usual wake-up time. Lying in bed and staring at the ceiling, he silently cursed his internal clock that didn't understand weekends or compensating for late nights. It did no good. Regardless of how much he wanted to, he wasn't going to fall back asleep.

With a groan, he sat up and scrubbed at his face with his palms. He needed a shave, but that could wait, he decided after a moment. His muscles felt tight from too little sleep. He stood and went through his morning stretches, but he still felt sluggish. "Well, fuck," he muttered, changing into heavy sweat pants and a thick sweatshirt. He pulled on his running shoes and went in search of his gloves and hat. It looked like he was going for a run.

The sight of Dany asleep on his couch drew him up short. Dany looked far too comfortable wrapped up in Frank's spare blanket. With a wicked grin, Frank went into the kitchenette that was separated from the living room by a half wall and grabbed a pot. He dropped it on the floor with a loud clatter, smothering a laugh when Dany nearly hit the ceiling.

"Wha—?" Dany said, looking around with wild eyes.

"Sorry," Frank said, holding up the pan. "I dropped it."

"What time is it?" Dany asked, peering toward the dark window.

"Six," Frank replied.

"What the hell are you doing awake at six in the morning?" Dany complained. "We didn't even come home until after two."

"Doesn't matter how late I stay out," Frank said. "I never sleep past six."

"I bet I could think of something that would help," Dany muttered.

"What's that?" Frank asked.

"A long, thorough fucking," Dany retorted. "You'd be too worn out to wake up early."

"And where am I going to find someone to do that?" Frank asked flippantly.

"I'm available," Dany joked. At least Frank hoped he was joking because if he was serious, Frank was a goner.

"Thanks, but no thanks," Frank said immediately. "I like my job too much to screw it up by screwing around."

"Did Jean-Paul give you the sex and cars speech too?" Dany asked with a huge yawn.

"What speech?" Frank asked.

"The sex and cars speech," Dany repeated. "When he told me he'd arranged for you to come for a test drive, he gave me a lecture about how sex and cars don't mix and that it didn't matter if you were gay and unattached, I wasn't allowed to get involved with you."

"He didn't say anything like that to me," Frank said, baffled at the conversation.

"That's odd," Dany said. "He must have figured you'd be too worried about your job to do anything stupid."

"And you aren't worried about yours?" Frank asked, feeling like he'd crossed into the Twilight Zone.

"Nah," Dany said. "The sponsors like me too much for that. I'd have to screw up a whole lot more than just messing around with a co-driver before they'd drop me."

"So you'd just throw me to the wolves?"

"Wait," Dany said. "What are you talking about? We haven't done anything to get us in trouble, anyway. Unless I was a whole lot drunker than I thought last night."

Frank waved aside Dany's last comment. "But if something went wrong, you'd just let me take the blame? I thought we were a team."

"We are a team," Dany said. "It's too early in the morning for this conversation because I don't understand why you're upset."

Frank didn't either, honestly, but he wasn't going to tell Dany that. "You just said I should be worried about my job, but you didn't need to be."

"I didn't say you should be worried about your job," Dany insisted. "Or if I did, I didn't mean it that way. I said Jean-Paul must have figured you'd be too worried about your job to mess around with me. I'm not going to do anything to screw up our partnership because I've never driven the way I do with you as my navigator, and we're still learning our way around each other. I can only imagine what it will be like in six months or six years. No way am I letting anything screw that up. Not the sponsors, not Jean-Paul. Not even me."

Somewhat mollified, if no less confused, Frank said, "How would you screw it up?"

"My track record at relationships sucks," Dany said bluntly. "I can sleep around and fuck anything that walks with no problem, but when it comes to actually having a relationship that lasts beyond a night or two… well, let's just say they're few and far between."

"You travel so much, it's no surprise," Frank replied immediately. "That's part of the sport. Anyone you were with would have to be free to travel with you or else be very understanding of the time you're gone."

"If that's all it were, there are ways around it," Dany said. "Each rally only takes a week at the most, at least in terms of the time I'd have to be there. Time to drive the course once to clean up our notes on the courses that let us, and then the actual two or three days of the race. I could fly more instead of traveling with Isa and the car so I'd be home more in between the races. It's not the travel. It's me. I have a habit of sabotaging myself. I don't do it on purpose, but I can't seem to stop doing it anyway. Jean-Paul knows that, and he also knows my common sense doesn't always win out over my dick. That's why he lectured me. So I'd know he was watching and that he didn't want any funny business between us."

"Has this been a problem before?" Frank asked, still not entirely sure how he felt about the sudden turn in the conversation.

"Not with my co-drivers, if that's what you mean," Dany said with a grimace. "Christophe was a fabulous co-driver, but he was quite a bit older and happily married, proof that it is possible to have a relationship even while you're driving full time. Xavier was a disaster from beginning to end, so that certainly wasn't an option."

"So why did he think it would be a problem now?" Frank pressed, sure there was more to this than Dany was telling him.

"Because you're young, gay, and attractive," Dany said. "And you're around all the time. There's an incredible intimacy to a good driving team. We have to get in each other's heads and stay there to be successful out on the courses. You saw it with the simulator. I couldn't see the problem, but you were able to get in my head and figure out what I was doing wrong. I listened and followed your advice, and we solved the problem. Can you imagine the explosions that kind of chemistry could create in bed?"

Frank had no problem imagining it since he'd spent far too many nights lying in bed doing exactly that. He'd known it was an impossible dream even before this conversation, but it seemed to have gotten even more out of reach as the morning went on.

"No point in imagining it since it won't ever happen," Frank said hoarsely. "I'm going for a run. Go back to sleep if you want. I'll be quiet when I come back in."

"It's six thirty in the morning," Dany muttered. "It's still dark outside."

"Not that dark," Frank said. "I do this every morning. I'll be fine."

Dany grumbled a little more, but he pulled himself up off the couch. "Give me ten minutes to wake up and some running clothes. I'll go with you."

Frank cursed under his breath, but he went back into his room and pulled out another pair of sweats. He was pretty sure the morning couldn't get any weirder, but he wasn't sure he should even think that for fear of something even stranger happening. Returning to the living room, he had to swallow around the lump of desire in his throat as Dany stripped off the jeans he had worn the night before, replacing them with the sweat pants Frank handed him. Fortunately for Frank's equilibrium, Dany wore a T-shirt beneath his sweater so all Frank got a glimpse of was strong arms rather than a full bare chest.

"Put on a hat and gloves if you have them," Frank said. "It's pretty frigid in the mornings until the sun comes up all the way."

"It's frigid even then," Dany retorted. "It snowed yesterday, in case you'd forgotten."

Frank hadn't forgotten, but he had to do something to stop himself from jumping Dany right there. Conversation seemed the sanest option. "Do you have a hat and gloves or should I try to dig some up for you?"

"I've got gloves," Dany said. "I don't think I even own a hat."

Frank shook his head and went back to his bedroom one more time, rummaging through his bottom drawer for an extra hat. He tossed it at Dany as he went back into the living room. "I don't want to hear it from Isa or Jean-Paul if you get sick."

"It snowed yesterday and you're dragging me out for a run," Dany reminded him. "You'll definitely hear it if I get sick."

"I'm not dragging you anywhere," Frank insisted as they walked toward the door. "I told you I was going for a run. You're the one who decided to come along."

"Details, details," Dany said with a roll of his eyes. "If you weren't going for a run in the first place, it never would have occurred to me."

The air was as cold as Frank had expected it to be, but after living in Canada all his life, he'd gotten used to winter weather. Compared to the temperatures he ran in there, this was practically balmy. Dany obviously didn't agree if the way he muttered under his breath as they started to run was any indication. Frank ignored him and settled into a comfortable pace, fast enough to get his blood moving and clear his head without pushing him to the point of breathlessness, which could be dangerous in cold temperatures. "Breathe through your nose," he warned Dany. "You can hurt your lungs otherwise."

Dany glared at him, but Frank noticed that he followed directions. They wended their way through the narrow streets of the old section of town. Frank was tempted to head out toward the outskirts of town and the country roads, but he had no idea what kind of a runner Dany was, and it was too cold to get out there and not be able to get back. By the time they had circled back toward Frank's apartment, Frank had warmed up nicely, all the cobwebs in his brain from lack of sleep and the alcohol the night before burning away from the exercise. Dany looked more alert as well, although he needed a shave. Frank hid a grin at the thought that the scruffy look suited him. Dany prided himself on being suave and polished when he was in the public eye, but Frank suspected he'd be even more popular with the ladies if they could see him like this. Then again, maybe Frank would keep that to himself. Dany was popular enough as it was.

That thought brought a frown to Frank's face. Here in Clermont-Ferrand, where he was a bit of a celebrity but also a local boy, Dany had behaved circumspectly most of the time, at least in Frank's presence, but Frank had followed Dany's career. He knew what would happen when the rallies started up again and they were away from home. He wasn't looking forward to it.

CHAPTER
SEVEN

THE roads in Sweden were as bad as Daniel had feared they would be as he and Frank drove the recce car through the course for the second day, trying to solidify their notes on road conditions so they would be ready for the race that started tomorrow. They couldn't push the speed limit at all today, which was one reason they were driving a standard road car instead of the race car, or they risked being disqualified, but even if it hadn't been against the rules, Daniel wouldn't have pushed it in this car on icy, unfamiliar roads.

"Tomorrow is going to be a bitch," he groaned to Frank as they navigated a sharp turn. "Left bend, s5. We're last because I didn't finish last season, and what little traction any fresh snow will give us on this ice will be long gone by the time we get our turn."

"Yeah, but the other twenty cars ahead of you will have melted some of the ice too," Frank said, checking his notes against Daniel's directions. "We'll have to be careful, but it's not an impossible task, and if it doesn't snow tonight, the early racers won't have any advantage either."

"Right bend, s1, no shoulder," Daniel dictated as they went around the next curve. The trees were so close to the edge of the road here that he wouldn't be able to cut the corner at all. Even at the slow speed, the car skidded on the ice. "*Merde*, this is going to be a hellish drive at speed."

"We don't have to break records," Frank said soothingly. "All we have to do is stay within striking distance of the leaders, and since we're last tomorrow, we'll know the time to beat."

"Why are you so damn calm?"

"Because you aren't," Frank replied. "If I weren't, we'd both be a wreck, and that would almost certainly lead to one. Now, calm down and concentrate on the road. Watch the race line on this curve. It's like what we had problems with back in November."

Daniel remembered. "Make it s3 instead of s2 if you haven't already," he directed. "The slower speed through the curve will cost less time than wiping out."

Frank's pencil scratched over the paper as Daniel's thoughts drifted back to the rather odd morning after they had finally broken his block on this particular configuration of curves. Daniel had given up trying to figure out what was happening between them. They continued to work together far more smoothly than Daniel could have anticipated, making him wonder when the explosion would happen. No partnership was ever seamless. It wasn't possible, which meant he and Frank were due for a blowup of some kind. He only hoped it didn't happen in the middle of a race. In the meantime, he lived with this sense of anticipation, not for the blowup, but for something else, something he couldn't put his finger on. He had no idea if Frank felt it, too, but since he couldn't explain it even to himself, he hadn't tried asking Frank about it.

"That's it," Frank said as they drove across the finish line for the last stage. "I'll clean the notes up tonight. Tomorrow should be relatively easy, with the shakedown in the morning and the ceremonial start tomorrow afternoon, followed by the first super special stage in the arena. Get some sleep tonight."

"I don't mess around before a race," Daniel snapped. "There's too much at stake, including our lives if there's a bad crash. I'm not going to do anything stupid."

"I didn't mean that," Frank said, the deep breath he took annoying Daniel even more for some reason. "You complained about not sleeping well the last few nights. That's what made me say it."

Daniel wasn't convinced, but he let it go. He didn't need an argument between them before the first stages of the rally. They had too much riding on the race. One race wasn't enough to make or break the season, but Daniel didn't want to start the year in the hole if he could help it. He wanted the podium, even if he ended up in second or third place. "Sorry I snapped," he said, although he wasn't sure how sincere his apology sounded. "I'm always tense before a race, and the first race of the year is the worst."

"And we haven't had any true race experience as a team, which only adds to it," Frank said. "I get it, but taking it out on me won't help."

"At this point, you'd do best to leave me alone for the night," Daniel said. "I know you're trying to help, but all it'll do now is annoy me, and that doesn't help either of us. I'm going to have one drink, eat dinner, and go to bed."

"Come for a run with me in the morning," Frank suggested. "It'll help work off some of the nervous energy."

Daniel doubted that, but it was only the second time Frank had invited him for a run. "What time? We have to be at the parc ferme by nine for the shakedown run."

"So we run at seven, back by seven thirty which gives us time to shower and eat, and still leave here by eight thirty to meet Isa," Frank proposed.

Daniel shuddered, but he could see the wisdom in Frank's suggestion. "All right, I'll meet you in the hotel lobby at seven."

"You aren't going to join the team for dinner?" Frank asked.

Daniel hadn't planned on it. He never had, even when he was racing with Christophe, because he'd wanted that quiet time to go over the next day's stages in his head until he could drive them in his sleep, but he hesitated now. "I guess I could," he said slowly. "I usually have dinner in my room and go over the pace notes again. Tomorrow is just the super special stage, but I still want to get things fixed in my head after the recce today, and the longer I wait, the harder that is."

"Come to dinner," Frank cajoled. "I'll go over the pace notes with you after that. You have to eat."

"Okay," Daniel agreed after a moment. "Let me take a shower, and I'll meet you at the restaurant."

DINNER had been far more enjoyable than Daniel expected, but the real revelation had come after dinner, when Frank helped him go over the pace notes. He had driven the course as part of the recce period to create the pace notes from the road book, but more than once, Frank's perceptions or memories of the course differed from his. They had stopped and discussed the details until they agreed on the layout of the road and shoulders and on the best strategy for attacking the race given the road conditions. It was a new experience for Daniel, and it made him wonder how many of the problems he'd had with Xavier might have been avoided if they could have communicated this way, except that he'd never had enough trust in Xavier's perceptions to revise his mental picture based on the other man's comments. That wasn't an issue with Frank. Frank had proven willing to listen and learn as well as to insist when necessary, and his insight in the simulators and on the practice courses they'd done had been invaluable.

As he lay in bed that night, he ran through the next day's stages in his head one more time with far more confidence that he'd felt in ages, certainly since Christophe retired, but probably even longer than that. He drifted off to sleep in the middle of mapping a stage in his mind and slept without waking until his alarm went off at ten 'til seven the next morning.

As he dressed in his winter running gear, Daniel pondered the night before once more. Meeting Frank in the lobby of the hotel, he threw his arm around his co-driver. "We have a new pre-race ritual," he declared. "I slept better last night than I do anywhere but my own bed in Clermont-Ferrand."

"Really?" Frank asked. "That's good."

"It is good," Daniel said. "Come on, let's run."

"So what made the difference?" Frank asked as they puffed their way through the streets of Karlstad.

"I think because by the time we were done talking, I didn't have any questions left in my head about the stages," Daniel said. "Usually I go over and over and over the roads in my mind, trying to make sure I've got everything exactly right, but our conversation did that for me already. When I lay down to sleep, all the noise in my head that usually keeps me awake before a race was gone. I fell asleep by ten and didn't move until the alarm went off this morning."

"That's good," Frank said. "You'll be in top form today, then, because you're rested."

"I certainly hope so," Daniel said, picking up the pace a little now that his muscles had started to warm up against the cold. He would be glad for the exercise when the adrenaline kicked in during the race, tightening all his muscles and sharpening his reflexes. The roads beneath the ice were gravel, which was reigning world champion Ryan Michaels's preferred medium for driving. If Daniel was going to give him a run for his money according to their plan, he'd have to be at his absolute best for the next three days.

They finished their run and parted for showers and breakfast, meeting back up in time to head to the parc ferme for the shakedown run and the rest of their day. Isabelle met them at the garage. "I've checked everything out. It all looks good. The tires have metal studs so you'll have some traction even on the ice, but it's still gravel beneath so watch yourself on the turns."

"I know, Isabelle," Daniel said with a long-suffering sigh. This wasn't the first time he'd run a race in Sweden or on icy gravel.

"Let's get suited up," Frank said, ending Daniel's staring match with his sister. Daniel sent Frank a grateful smile, ducking into the garage to pull on the flameproof overalls he wore over his clothes while he was driving. It made for some miserable drives in the desert heat of Jordan and Mexico, but he'd be glad for the extra layer in the arctic temperatures in Sweden. Twenty-five degrees below zero was miserable no matter how many layers he had on.

When they were dressed and had their helmets on, they headed toward the start of the shakedown stage. They waited their turn to run the course, Daniel's nerves kicking up as they sat in the queue. Finally their turn came, the start signal flashing for them to go, and Daniel hit the accelerator, pulling the paddle shifter to send the car through the gears. The tires worked as Isabelle had promised, giving them traction even on the icy curves. Daniel kept the speed high but within their normal parameters. This wasn't about having the fastest time but about handling the car in race conditions. Nobody cared if he came in faster or slower than anyone else at this point. Isabelle would want to know how the car handled, how the engine sounded, whether there were problems with the acceleration or the brakes or anything else technical, so he concentrated on that and the sound of Frank's voice in his ear, telling him what to expect.

They finished the run in a respectable thirteen minutes. Daniel didn't even look to see what times the other drivers had gotten. He'd gotten what he needed.

"How did it feel?" Isabelle asked when they reached the service park again.

"Everything felt fine," Daniel replied. "The tire studs made a huge difference from yesterday."

"Good," Isabelle said. "I'll check everything once more and get the car ready for tonight. Get some food and relax a bit before the ceremonial start. I'll see you back here at four to line up?"

"We'll be here," Frank said before Daniel could snap at his sister again. "Come on, Dany," Frank continued, drawing Daniel away. "Let's find some lunch."

Daniel grumbled all the way to the bistro where they decided to eat. Frank let him, thankfully.

"Hey," Frank said, nudging Daniel's foot beneath the table once they were settled, "why do you let her get to you that way?"

"Because she's an annoying bitch who thinks I'm still twelve years old and can't remember to tie my shoes before I walk out of the house," Daniel muttered.

"She doesn't think that," Frank insisted. "She wants you to do your best during the rally, and so she double checks details, but that doesn't mean she thinks you're incompetent."

"Not incompetent," Daniel allowed, "but too young and immature to do without her constant supervision. I'm surprised she didn't remind me not to have a glass of wine with lunch. She usually does. Like I don't have the good sense not to drink before a race."

"If I talk to her and get her to tone it down a bit, will you lighten up on her too?" Frank bargained.

"If you can get her to do that, I'll be your slave for life," Daniel said, the words out before he could consider the wisdom of such a broad offer.

"That could be interesting," Frank teased. "Too bad I can't do anything… fun with the offer."

Daniel bit back a groan, his blood rushing south at the implications of Frank's comment. *Sex and cars don't mix*, he chanted silently, but with adrenaline already kicking through him from the shakedown run and with the tension high before the super special stage tonight, he had more trouble than usual convincing his unruly body to listen. They took their time over lunch, enjoying the food, even if it was more reminiscent of what they would get at home rather than local dishes. When they were finished, Daniel sighed. "I guess we should head to the driver autograph session, shouldn't we?"

Frank laughed. "You should head to the session. No one will care about getting my autograph. Maybe this time next year if we do well as far as the championship is concerned, but I'm an unknown at the moment. I'll go hang out with Isabelle and see if I can get her off your case a bit. I'll see you at four to get ready for the start."

Daniel sighed again. Frank was right, but he still felt abandoned. Rolling his eyes at his own foolishness, he pasted on his best smile and went to sign autographs for an hour or two.

AS SOON as Daniel could get away without appearing rude, he left the signing. Even being harangued by Isabelle would be better than mindlessly signing autographs for people who didn't speak French or German. He spoke a little English, but in Sweden, their English was as broken as his, not exactly conducive to easy conversation. Not that signing autographs was the time for any truly meaningful conversation, but most of the time, he could barely even catch their names. He signed photos and posters and other merchandise with a determined smile, reminding himself that public relations was part of his job as well, even if it was a part he hated. He appreciated the support of the fans and was happy to give them a good show on the race course, but the rest always felt fake to him.

Isabelle glared at him when he came in, but she didn't say anything as he pulled all his protective gear back on and joined Frank under the hood. "How's everything looking?"

"Perfect as always," Frank said. "Isa wouldn't send us out to race in anything less. How was the signing?"

Daniel rolled his eyes. "Tedious, but it's over. Now we have to get through the ceremonial start, and then we can actually start the race. I'm ready."

"Me too," Frank said. "At least we'll be early in the ceremonial start since it's in reverse order from the actual starts. That way we'll have plenty of time for dinner before we have to be back for the super special stage."

"I ate so much at lunch that I doubt I'll be hungry," Daniel said, "not with my nerves kicking in."

"You mean you don't want to try *surströmming* for dinner?" Frank teased.

Daniel grimaced at the thought of the fermented herring dish. He knew it was a local specialty, but he couldn't get past the smell to actually taste it. "*Merci*," he said with a shake of his head. "I'll have a sandwich or something to hold me over and eat dinner after the stage is over tonight."

They puttered around in the garage a little longer before heading out for the ceremonial start. At least there, they would have translators if the emcee for the event didn't speak French. Daniel pasted on his best racing smile and waited his turn in line.

The interviewer spoke English, fortunately, saving Daniel from having to rely on a translator, even if his own grasp of the language was a bit sketchy.

"Do you have a plan for the rally?" the interviewer asked.

"Do our best on each stage and don't crash," Daniel joked, his accent thick. "Hopefully stay near the leader so we can score points for the championship."

"Ice and gravel haven't been your best combination in the past," the interviewer went on. "Have you worked on that this winter?"

"We drove many courses in Auvergne and the Alps," Daniel replied.

"You have a new co-driver this year."

"Yes," Daniel said, his smile becoming more genuine. "Frank Dufour. We will do our best this year. I think we will surprise people."

"Good luck, and we'll be watching for those surprises."

DANIEL hated waiting. He wanted to be near the top of the roster during a race so he could get the stages over with rather than watching the leader boards shift for nearly two hours before he even got a shot at the first course. When his turn finally came, Michaels was ahead by a full two seconds, a significant time for a stage that only lasted two minutes. The other stages would be longer, but Daniel was determined to close that gap. He didn't really expect to win on the ice and gravel, but he intended to make Michaels work for the win.

The signal flashed to indicate his start and Frank's voice sounded in his ear, talking him through the stage. He drove fast but not overly recklessly, not here in the first stage. Yes, he had a leader to catch, but he didn't have to beat the time, just stay within striking distance to take advantage of any mistakes Michaels might make later. When he crossed the finish line for the stage, he looked at the time. Less than one second behind.

"How did we do that?" Daniel asked, turning to stare at Frank.

"You drove well," Frank replied, his voice coming through the helmet's earpiece. "And maybe Michaels didn't. We won't know until we get back to the garage where we can look at the footage. Come on, let's get some sleep. As well as we did tonight, we'll be an early starter tomorrow. We have to get to Hagfors by seven, and it's an hour and a half drive from Karlstad."

Daniel nodded as he drove the car back to the parc ferme. "Can we go over the pace notes for the first of tomorrow's stages first? I'll sleep better if it's clear in my head."

"After the way you drove tonight, we can talk pace notes all you want," Frank promised. "We can discuss them all the way to Hagfors tomorrow too."

"Thanks," Daniel said as he dropped the car off with Isabelle. "For everything."

CHAPTER EIGHT

"THERE'S no fresh snow this morning," Frank reported as they drove north to Hagfors for the service park and the day's stages, "so the roads should feel very much like they did yesterday except for the better traction from the racing tires. The trick here is going to be not making mistakes. We don't have to beat everyone else's times. We have to stay in the race and place high enough to get points toward the championship."

"Yeah," Daniel said, "the winter rally almost always goes to one of the Nordic drivers, although Michaels took the stage last night."

"A two-minute stadium course that was more showboating than anything else," Frank scoffed. "I know he's good on gravel, and he's proven himself on ice in the past, but it isn't a given that he'll win. He's had some pretty spectacular crashes on the ice too. Everyone makes mistakes sometimes."

"Let's hope we don't make any this time," Daniel said.

"We won't," Frank replied, his voice confident. "Do you want to go over the pace notes for the first three stages again today, before the regrouping and service park at lunch time?"

"Yes," Daniel said. "Going through them before the race helped keep things clear in my head for yesterday. Let's not mess with success."

They spent the rest of the drive to Hagfors to meet Isabelle and her mechanics, as well as the other drivers and race officials, discussing the stages to come. Isabelle shooed them away from the car the moment the service park time began, the four mechanics going over every inch of the car with as much care as if they hadn't seen it in ages. Daniel would have made a comment about Isabelle second-guessing herself or not being sure she'd done the job right the first time, but she'd been surprisingly civil last night after the super special stage so Daniel hoped maybe Frank's conversation with her had helped. He wouldn't start anything if she didn't.

Forty minutes later, the race officials called for the drivers to start lining up for the first stage. Daniel strapped in and took his place behind Ryan Michaels's Mitsubishi Lancer Evolution X. Daniel would start two minutes after Michaels did, enough that he wouldn't have to worry about catching up with the American, not at the speeds they'd be driving, unless Michaels had a wreck or technical problems that slowed him down. He'd be happy with not losing time.

Michaels disappeared in a spray of snow, and Daniel drove into position, eyes fixed on the starter. It flashed one minute and started the countdown. He waited, foot hovering over the accelerator as the count continued. As it neared zero, he gunned the engine, foot still hard on the brake. The moment the counter hit zero, he released the brake, Frank's voice in his ear guiding him through the bends. The car skidded beneath him on the bends, but their practice in the Alps held him in good stead and he managed the bends with enough control not to lose time. He clipped a snow bank on one curve, but it didn't slow him down by more than a fraction of a second as he manhandled the car back to the race line and around the next bend. He'd have a second chance at that stretch of road this afternoon. Hopefully he wouldn't make the same mistake a second time, but he'd worry about that during the break for lunch. For now he had to concentrate on the road in front of him, the car beneath his hands, and Frank's voice talking him through the course.

Eleven minutes and thirty-three seconds after they started, they crossed the flying finish. "How'd we do?" Daniel asked Frank breathlessly as he slowed the car to normal speeds and started the trek to the next starting line.

"We won't know until lunch, but it felt good," Frank said, "other than the one snow bank. You ready for the next stage?"

"Bring it on," Daniel said, flashing Frank a cocky grin as he navigated the narrow country roads, glad of the metal spikes on the tires even at normal speeds.

Michaels was already there ahead of them when they reached the second starting line of the day. They had a few minutes before the start of the next stage, so Daniel got out of the car to stretch a bit, hissing at the cold temperatures.

"Having problems there, Leroux?" Michaels sneered from his car.

"Not me," Daniel shot back, stretching his back a little.

"Don't worry," Michaels added. "You won't be eating my dust for long."

"No, you'll be eating mine," Daniel retorted, finishing his stretches and returning to the car. "His ass is mine," he said to Frank as he climbed back in the car.

Frank laughed. "Somehow I don't think you mean that the way it sounded."

Daniel scowled at his co-driver. "We can't let him win the championship. Regardless of how he does during this rally, he's going down for the season."

"You bet, boss," Frank agreed. "Are you set for the next stage?"

"All we need is the green light," Daniel replied as Michaels's start time arrived and he sped off down the course. Daniel pulled the car into position and prepared to tackle the third stage.

By the time they returned to the service park at Hagfors for lunch, four stages of the rally complete, Daniel was ready for a break. His back had tensed up from the constant struggle to hold the car on course. While Isabelle checked the car over again, changing the tires and refilling the gas and doing everything else that needed to be done, Daniel went inside the garage in search of coffee, a bathroom, and somewhere warm to take off his overalls and relax for a bit.

Frank followed him inside, handing him coffee as he came out of the restroom. "You doing okay?"

"A little stiff," Daniel admitted. "Between the cold and the tension of racing, I'll need some paracetemol before we go back out."

"Take some now," Frank said, "so it has time to work before the afternoon stages. We're still in second place, but Asikainen is gaining on us and Garza is only a little behind him."

"How far ahead did Michaels pull?" Daniel asked, digging in the first aid kit for a pain reliever.

"He's four seconds ahead of us, with Asikainen two seconds behind us," Frank reported. "Brushing the snow bank cost us a bit."

"Could you tell what happened?" Daniel asked. "Did I misjudge the race line?"

"No, I think you misjudged the skid," Frank replied. "Isa's got the video if you want to look at it."

"After I eat something," Daniel said. "My stomach is growling something fierce from all the adrenaline. Then we'll talk strategy for the afternoon stages."

BY THE time they finished the day's stages at Hagfors and headed back to Karlstad for another super special stage, Daniel could feel the analgesic wearing off again. "I'm glad we're second for the super special stage tonight," he admitted to Frank. "My back is killing me."

"Take a hot bath when you get back to the hotel, and then I'll give you a back rub if you want," Frank offered. "My mom had chronic back pain growing up, but we couldn't afford a massage therapist, so I learned quite a bit in order to help her."

The idea of Frank's hands on his bare back was enticing enough to make Daniel wonder if it was really a good idea, but they had two more days of driving, and he had no intention of retiring from the race because he was worried about keeping his libido under control. He'd simply have to deal with any tension on his own once Frank went back to his room.

"That would be fantastic," Daniel replied. "Anything to get the knots out of my spine."

"It's one of the hazards of the job," Frank said with a smile. "You spend so much time tensed up driving, not to mention the abuse your body goes through in a crash. Sometimes I think it's a miracle we're all still walking at the end of the day."

"Some days, I'm not," Daniel laughed, "but we didn't crash today, so today it just hurts a little."

It hurt more than a little, but Daniel didn't want Isabelle to find out and insist on taking him to a doctor tonight. He needed to sleep so he'd be awake enough to drive tomorrow. They had fallen to third place, half a second behind Asikainen, but Daniel had plans to regain his position tomorrow.

"Let's see if we can make it not hurt at all," Frank proposed. "We have an hour for dinner when we get back to Karlstad. I could work on it a little then."

"I'd only mess it up again during the last stage tonight," Daniel demurred.

"Maybe, but there's nothing that says I can only give you one massage a day," Frank countered, "and if you're more relaxed going into the stage tonight, you might drive better."

"Let's see how long dinner takes," Daniel said. "If there's time, I'll take you up on the offer."

THEY reached Karlstad and finished dinner with half an hour to spare. "I don't have any good massage cream with me," Frank said as they sat in the garage waiting for the next stage, "but I'll do the best I can."

"How do you want me?" Dany asked.

All sorts of images flashed through Frank's head at that question, but he pushed them aside. "Straddle the chair and lean on the back so it supports your arms," he directed. "You'll be able to relax your back that way so I can actually help a bit."

"It's awfully cool to take my shirt off, even in here," Dany said.

Frank grinned. "That's fine. I'll work through the fabric for now. We'll save the deep stuff for tonight after the race."

Dany looked a little nervous at that, but Frank just kept grinning, and eventually Dany settled into the chair. It wasn't as supportive as a massage chair would have been, but Frank didn't keep one of those in his back pocket. He'd make do with what he could get at this point.

He ran his hands down the length of Dany's spine, kneading lightly. "Tell me when I hit a tender spot," he said. "With the cloth in the way, I'm not going to feel the knots as well as I could with bare skin."

With his hands on Dany's back, Frank felt the telltale shiver that went through the other man. *Now isn't that interesting?* he thought. When he hit the base of Dany's ribcage, the hiss that escaped told Frank all he needed to know. "Try to relax into my hands. If you tense up against what I'm doing, it will only hurt worse."

"I've had massages before," Dany retorted.

"Then why are you jumping like I goosed you?" Frank asked, beginning to work the tense muscles in earnest. Dany groaned softly but didn't reply.

Taking the silence as consent, Frank worked down to the waistband of Dany's pants and back up to his ribs again, putting as much pressure on the tense muscles as he could at that angle. He would do better later, when he could stretch Dany out on the bed and get rid of the shirt, but this would have to do for now. He felt the moment the tension released beneath his hands, both in the muscles and in Dany's audible sigh.

"Wow, you're really good at that."

Frank smiled. "I try. We've got a couple more minutes. Should I keep going?"

"No, I'm fine," Dany said with a shake of his head. "I should get my overalls back on, and we should find Isabelle. She might have last-minute updates for us."

Frank suspected that was an excuse, but he let it go, ending his contact with Dany's back.

THEY moved back into second place, although only by a half second, by the end of the second super special stage. "You like the arena," Frank commented as they drove back to the garage.

Daniel shrugged. "Because it's short and in an arena, a lot of the drivers show off and don't drive as cleanly as they would on a longer stage. It's like they don't even take it seriously. I take every drive seriously because I don't want it to be the one that causes us to lose a race or worse."

"It was a compliment," Frank said soothingly, which only irritated Daniel more. He knew what he was doing, but apparently so did Frank, refusing to let Daniel pick a fight. The backrub in the garage lingered in Daniel's mind along with Frank's intentions of giving him a better one once they got back to the hotel. Daniel had barely survived the first one, sitting up and with his clothes on. He wasn't sure the second one, half undressed and lying flat on a bed in a room with a lock, was such a good idea.

Except that his back hurt and he didn't think a paracetemol or two would take care of it. They still had two full days of racing left, and Frank's massage had helped in the garage. They left the car in the parc ferme. Daniel knew Isabelle would be somewhere muttering about not being able to get her hands on the car that night, but they'd have a service park in the morning in Hagfors before they started the second day's racing. She'd have to make do with that.

Driving a street car back to the hotel where they were staying in Karlstad, Daniel twisted in his seat each time they stopped, trying to convince the muscles in his back to relax. If he could get them to stop hurting on his own, he could thank Frank for the offer and go to his room alone.

"Stretching can only do so much," Frank said from the seat next to him. "You can't stretch, especially in a car, all the ways your muscles would need to in order to relax fully. When we get to the hotel, take a shower, as hot as you can stand, and then call me. I'll come to your room and finish what I started earlier."

Daniel hoped the darkness inside the car hid the grimace on his face. "Thanks," he said tightly. He'd jerk off in the shower. Maybe that would help.

AN HOUR later, facedown on his bed in loose sweatpants, Daniel was pretty sure it hadn't helped at all. Frank straddled the back of his thighs as he worked a strong smelling ointment into the sore muscles with strong, determined fingers. The massage felt like heaven. There was absolutely no denying that. Daniel could feel the little points of pain giving in beneath Frank's determined assault.

Unfortunately, as the pain faded, Daniel became progressively more aware of the very warm, very male body that pressed his legs into the mattress, the weight disappearing from his thighs periodically as Frank leaned forward and used his forearm on Daniel's back. That was even worse because every time he did that, Daniel had a flash of Frank kneeling over him on hands and knees, the perfect position for more intimate activities.

After one particularly drawn-out moment of Frank's arm and elbow pressing hard against a tense knot in his shoulder, Daniel gave in to the need rising in him and squirmed a little on the bed, trying to relieve the awkward position of his cock beneath his body.

"Are you all right?" Frank asked immediately. "I'm not hurting you, am I?"

"No, it doesn't hurt," Daniel said, his voice tight. "I was just trying to get more comfortable on the bed."

Frank rocked back until he was standing on his knees, still straddling Daniel but not putting any weight on his body. "Get comfortable again. The massage might hurt a little in places, but the rest of you shouldn't hurt."

Daniel lifted up a bit and settled on the bed again with everything at a better angle.

"Ready?" Frank asked when Daniel had stopped moving.

Daniel nodded, waiting almost impatiently for the hot press of Frank's hands on his skin again.

Frank worked on Daniel's back for awhile longer, until Daniel was floating on the sensation and relaxing in a way he hadn't in months. The feeling of Frank rolling down the waistband of his sweats startled a squawk from his lips as he pushed up on one elbow to stare back at his co-driver.

"Relax," Frank said, "I'm not trying to molest you, but the muscles in your back end at the top of your ass. If I don't work all the way down to the base of your spine, the tension will climb right back up during the night. I swear, I'm not putting the moves on you. You'd think you'd never had a massage before."

Daniel scowled, but he subsided onto the bed. He'd had enough massages to know Frank was right, but that didn't make it any more comfortable to lie there with half his butt hanging out and his co-driver's, his very attractive co-driver's, hands rubbing over his skin.

Frank's hands stayed exactly where the pain was, not copping a feel, which reassured Daniel. They could do this. They could stick to Jean-Paul's edict and be friends without bringing sex into the equation, because no matter how tempted he was to roll over and pull Frank down on top of him, sex and cars couldn't mix, and Daniel wasn't about to do anything that would jeopardize the incredible chemistry he and Frank had on the circuit. Even with Christophe, he'd never been so fully in contention on a Nordic course during the winter. He and Frank had something too precious to risk. Now he simply had to convince his body of that fact.

CHAPTER
NINE

CLIMBING out of the car at the service park after the second day's morning stages, Frank checked out their time. They'd fallen behind Michaels by nearly fifteen seconds, but they wouldn't know until Asikainen finished if that was enough to put them into third. He didn't think it would drop them into fourth given how far behind Garza had been at the end of the day yesterday, but it was always possible.

He glanced automatically in Dany's direction to see how his driver was walking at this point. He hadn't complained of his back bothering him yesterday until the end of the afternoon stages, but Frank didn't see any reason to wait that long today if he saw signs of distress. The better Dany felt, the better he would drive, and as challenging as today's stages were, they needed him in top form.

Memories of the night before flashed through Frank's mind, of Dany spread out on the bed beneath him, occasionally shifting restlessly. Frank had managed to keep his touch impersonal as he massaged, taking his cues from Dany's body language about what felt good, what hurt, and what was simply too much, but he had been ever so glad of the privacy of his own room when he had finished the massage. He never would have been able to sleep with Dany in the same room.

Dany seemed pretty comfortable at the moment as they headed into the garage to get out of the frigid wind.

"We've got to do better this afternoon," Dany said as soon as they were inside.

"We drove cleanly," Frank said. "You didn't miss any of the race lines. You kept the skid under control. It was a picture-perfect race."

"And yet we're falling farther and farther behind," Dany complained.

"Michaels is taking chances at every turn," Jean-Paul said, coming into the garage as they were talking. "So far they're paying off, but all it takes on a course like this one is one miscalculation and he's out of the race. There's a trick to winning a rally championship, you know, and it isn't winning every race. It's *finishing* every race in a respectable time. You aren't fifteen seconds behind during the last race of the season where beating him means the championship. This is the first race of the season. If you get the podium, even in third place, you're still well in the running for the championship. And if he makes a mistake because he's trying to beat you, then you'll end up with more points than him because of it. Don't end up with fewer points—or none—because you're the one who makes a mistake."

Jean-Paul handed Frank a sheet of paper. "Keep doing exactly what you're doing. Michaels might be in the lead, but look at that."

"What is it?" Frank asked, looking down at the table of numbers.

"Daniel's stage times on this rally from his previous runs. Instead of comparing him to Michaels this year, I compared him to himself in previous years," Jean-Paul explained. "It's not a perfect comparison because some of the stages have changed a little, but it will still give you an idea."

"Dany, look at this," Frank said as the numbers started to make sense in his head. "If I'm reading this right, you're running good minute and a half ahead of where you were in this rally at this point last year."

"Yeah, well, last year wasn't exactly a stellar performance," Dany complained.

"Okay, what year should I look at?"

"Three years ago," Dany said. "That's the highest I ever placed in Sweden."

Frank took a minute to find the appropriate column. "You're still twenty seconds faster than that year," Frank said as he followed the chart with his finger.

"Therefore," Jean-Paul said, fixing Dany with a hard stare, "you will keep doing exactly what you've been doing and not take any unnecessary risks. If you finish in the top five, you will still be easily in contention for the trophy because the rest of the rallies are in conditions you're far more comfortable with."

"Asikainen just finished his morning runs," Isabelle announced, joining them in the garage office.

"And?" Dany asked.

"And he beat both of you. He's two seconds ahead of Michaels at this point."

Dany cursed under his breath.

"I repeat," Jean-Paul said, "you will not take any unnecessary risks. You've competed with Michaels. You know how he'll react to this. He'll take it as a personal insult and push even harder, and if we're lucky, he'll make a mistake because of it. Even if he doesn't, fifteen points for third instead of eighteen points for second place will not make that big a difference. No points because you couldn't finish the race or because you put yourself so far behind with a spin-out will make a difference."

Frank was tempted to remind Jean-Paul that all the lectures in the world wouldn't matter when Dany was out there on the course, the one behind the wheel and in control of the car, but he held his tongue. He didn't want Jean-Paul to accuse him of encouraging reckless behavior. They'd have enough problems if Dany decided not to listen. Frank didn't want to make it worse.

"Let's get something to eat," Frank said, breaking the staring match between Dany and Jean-Paul. "We don't have all that long before we have to be back out on the road for the next stage, and we don't want a penalty for being late."

AFTER they'd wolfed down the sandwiches that were really all they had time to eat, Daniel loosened his overalls and bent at the waist, stretching his back and upper thighs. Frank's massage had helped. He wasn't nearly as stiff as he'd been at this point yesterday, but that didn't mean he should neglect his stretches. As he straightened, Frank's hand brushed across his lower back.

"Ça va?" Frank asked.

Daniel shivered from the unexpected touch. "I'm fine," he said shortly. He turned to escape Frank's hand and caught sight of his co-driver's face. Damn, he'd been sharper than he'd intended. "More than fine, actually," he said, consciously summoning a smile and a softer tone of voice. "Your massage last night did wonders. I always stretch between sets of stages so I don't tense up, but I can't remember when I last felt this good at lunchtime."

Frank glanced around the garage quickly, making Daniel do the same.

"What's up?" Daniel asked. "No one's here but us."

"Do you agree with what Jean-Paul said earlier about our strategy for the rest of the race?" Frank asked.

Daniel chuckled. "What a neutral way to ask the question. I see the logic of it, and the numbers he showed us are pretty impressive in terms of my performance here over the time I've been racing, but it goes against the grain not to push for a win when we're so close still. Seventeen seconds difference and we're already halfway through the rally. That's incredibly close."

Frank nodded. "So what are we going to do?"

"We're going to drive our best," Daniel said grimly. "We're going to do everything right and hope Michaels or Asikainen makes a mistake. And if we take third instead of second or first, we'll still be on the podium. We'll take chances when it really matters. Unless you had another suggestion?"

Frank shook his head. "We aren't going to win this race by taking chances. Not on these icy roads. We'll save that for Bulgaria or Germany or France when the asphalt is in our favor or for Japan and Great Britain when it comes down to the wire."

"I know," Daniel said, and he did, but it rankled to let Michaels and Asikainen beat him without doing everything he could to pass their times. Then the paper Jean-Paul had handed Frank caught his eye, and he picked it up and stared at it again. Every stage that had repeated from previous years, even the one where he clipped the snow bank on the first day, showed significant improvement over his times from the earlier races. He looked up at Frank and back down at the chart. Maybe he really was doing everything he could simply by listening to Frank.

"Let's go. We've got stages to run and a podium to hold onto. A clean run with no mistakes. That's what we're aiming for."

"That's what we'll do," Frank said, his voice so full of confidence that Daniel relaxed and went with it. Frank would tell him what to do, he'd do it, and they'd expand the gap with the drivers behind them and let Michaels and Asikainen do crazy stunts ahead of them. If they pulled them off, good for them, and if they didn't, all the better to win the rally.

"I WOULDN'T mind another massage if you have time," Dany said as they drove back to Karlstad after the afternoon stages. There wasn't a super special stage tonight, so once they'd finished their last stage for the day, they were done until the next day. Frank had been looking forward to a relaxed meal in a quiet restaurant and an early bedtime. Now it looked like he might have to amend the bedtime anyway.

"I have time," Frank said. "How badly does it hurt?"

"Not as bad as yesterday," Dany assured Frank, "but I'm stiff, and I don't want that to impact my driving tomorrow."

"We've got a full minute's lead over the next driver," Frank said.

"All it would take is one bad stage and that could disappear," Dany reminded him. "I'm not pushing for second, but I don't want to lose third if I can help it."

"And this is something we can do," Frank finished for him. "Okay. I was thinking about going out to dinner tonight, somewhere warm and quiet where I could have a beer—just one, I know, since we have to get up early again tomorrow—and relax a little. It's hard work sitting in the passenger seat."

Dany laughed, and Frank let it go, but in some ways, it was harder for him than anything else he did. He was a control freak and he knew it. It made him a good co-driver because he was obsessive about his notes and his accuracy, but it also meant he spent the entire race tensed because the car itself was out of his control. He needed to unwind.

"Do you want company?" Dany asked.

"I wouldn't say no," Frank replied, pleased at the invitation, "but I didn't know if you had other plans for the evening."

"With more stages tomorrow?" Dany laughed. "My plans are to go to bed early so I'll be ready for the last day. I can party tomorrow night."

"I've been eyeing a little bistro around the corner from the hotel," Frank suggested. "I haven't seen a lot of rally people going in and out of it, so we should be able to have dinner without constant interruptions."

"Sounds good to me," Dany replied. "I'll need a shower first."

"So will I," Frank said, ignoring the image that flashed through his head of Dany under a spray of water. He had to keep himself under control. *Sex and cars don't mix.*

THEY made it through dinner without any uncomfortable silences or overly telling looks, much to Frank's relief. He'd jerked off in the shower, hoping it would give him enough relief that he wouldn't get hard while he was massaging Dany's back after dinner, but the quiet intimacy of the restaurant and the casual assumption on the part of the waiter that they were a couple did nothing for Frank's peace of mind. It felt like a date, no matter how hard he tried to convince his unruly body otherwise.

As they walked back to the hotel, Frank wouldn't have been surprised to feel Dany's hand in his. Except, of course, for the fact that they weren't lovers. They were co-workers in a profession that required them to rely on each other completely, and adding sexual tension to that mix would only endanger both their lives.

"Go get comfortable," Frank told Dany as they entered the hotel. "I'll change as well and meet you in your room in about fifteen minutes."

"I don't need that long to get comfortable," Dany joked.

Frank glared at him mildly. "Maybe I do."

"Gonna jerk off first?" Dany asked.

Frank flushed but held Dany's gaze. "No, I'm going to call my mother. It's her birthday."

Dany had the good grace to blush. "Sorry. That was crude and uncalled for. Wish your mother a happy birthday from me as well. And take your time talking to her. My back will keep."

Frank nodded sharply, walking toward his room, the comfortable intimacy of the evening shattered by the crass comment. Was he that transparent in his interest in Dany? He thought he'd managed to keep it under control and out of Dany's notice, but maybe not, if Dany's comment was any indication. He let himself into his hotel room and changed clothes quickly into sweats that would be more comfortable for giving Dany a massage again as well as more likely to hide any reaction he had since they were loose. Sitting down on the bed, he pulled out his cell phone and called his mother.

The time difference meant that it was still mid-afternoon for her. They chatted for a few minutes about the lunch she'd had with her girlfriends and the plans his father had made for that evening. Frank apologized for not being there and told her to look for her birthday present in a few days. He'd sent it expedited, but it was still coming from Sweden.

"You didn't have to do that, *chéri*," she cooed.

"I know," Frank replied, smiling at the pleasure he could hear in her voice, "but I saw it in a shop window and knew you'd love it." Fortunately Dany hadn't been with him when he saw the beautiful red pleated fleece poncho in the window so he hadn't had to listen to the other man's teasing about buying women's clothing.

"Your sister's calling. I'm going to let you go because I know it's late over there," his mother said. "Sleep well tonight and drive safely tomorrow. You have a good driver this time, don't you?"

"Yes, Maman," Frank said, knowing his mother worried about Nadine, his sister, since her pregnancy had been fraught with complications. "I have a very good driver this time, and he knows about me already so that won't be a problem like the last time."

"Good," Mrs. Dufour said. "We'll cheer for you when you win tomorrow."

Frank didn't remind his mother that third place hardly counted as winning. As far as she was concerned, if he finished the race, he had won. Given how many teams didn't finish a rally each time, he supposed she was right. Last year, only three teams had completed all thirteen rallies. "We may not win big on this one, Maman," he said, "but you just wait until we get away from all this ice and snow. We'll be center stage on that podium more times than I've ever been before."

"That's good, Frank. That's really good," his mother said. "As long as you're happy and doing well, we're happy for you."

Frank thought of Dany waiting for him in the other room and smiled. "I *am* happy, Maman. I'll call again in a few days."

"*Bonne nuit, chéri*," she said as she ended the call.

Frank sat on the bed for a few minutes more, a smile on his face at his mother's faith in him. She'd like Dany, he thought, although she'd have a few choice words to say to him about keeping her baby safe. Chuckling as he imagined Dany's reaction to that, he rose and found the liniment he'd used on Dany's back and his keycard so he could get back in his room when he was done.

He found Dany's door propped open so he let himself in with a knock to announce his presence but without waiting for a verbal invitation. He found Dany stretched out on the bed already, his eyes closed. He paused for a moment to take in the sight on the bed. Dany's upper body was bare, revealing skin pale now from the months hidden beneath heavy sweaters and coats. It might not get quite as cold in Auvergne as it got in Sweden, but they certainly hadn't been out sunbathing either. Only Dany's face and hands showed the kiss of the sun still, from the weekends spent on the ski slopes and the days spent driving with no gloves and the sun beaming through the windshield of the car. He bore the proof of his active lifestyle in the wiry muscles that came in so useful as he fought to keep the car under his control when ice and gravel and inertia wanted to send it in a different direction. Frank had felt them under his hands the day before, but he'd focused primarily on Dany's lower back where the tension resided. He thought he'd see if Dany would let him do a more thorough job tonight, working his neck and shoulders as well.

"You still awake?" Frank asked softly, not wanting to disturb Dany if he'd fallen asleep waiting.

"Mhmm…."

Frank chuckled at the mumbled reply, but Dany lifted his head and opened his eyes, so Frank figured it was safe to approach the bed. "Get up for a second so I can pull the covers down," Frank instructed. "That way if you fall asleep, I can pull them over you on my way out and you won't even have to move again."

Dany turned lazily to one side, so Frank rolled his eyes and peeled down the sheet and duvet. Dany rolled back into the space, shivering a little. "Sheets are cold," he mumbled.

"Close your eyes and go to sleep," Frank ordered with a laugh. "I'll work on your back a bit and then let you rest."

Dany did as Frank said, relaxing onto the mattress as Frank climbed on the bed and straddled his thighs. Frank started with Dany's lower back again, noticing he didn't get a squawk tonight when he rolled down the waistband of Dany's pajamas to get at the base of his spine. It made Frank want to keep going, but that wasn't what he was here for. Concentrating on the task at hand, he massaged the muscles, relieved to find them much less tense than the night before, so he worked his way up Dany's spine to his shoulders, shifting so he straddled Dany's lower back now instead of his legs. Dany mumbled his pleasure as Frank started working on the tense shoulder and neck muscles and then down his arm. He lifted Dany's hand, threading their fingers together so he could work Dany's palm, the intimacy of the gesture almost too much for him. Gulping down a deep breath, he released Dany's hand and found a different way to hold the other one as he massaged that palm and fingers.

Sex and cars don't mix.

CHAPTER TEN

DANIEL tapped the steering wheel impatiently as they waited for the rally organizers to give him the signal for the ceremonial finish. Unlike the ceremonial start, only the top three cars participated in this bit of pomp and circumstance. Daniel could have wished he were two cars back in the line, but he was in the line, and that was already a huge achievement given his record on ice over his career. Michaels and Asikainen waited behind him, and since Michaels was directly behind them, that only put them three points apart in the championship standings. Asikainen was good, but he wouldn't hold on to his current first place ranking for long. Once they got away from the ice and snow—no snow in Jordan—Asikainen would lose the advantage he'd had here on his home turf. Finland was the only other rally where Asikainen would be a serious threat unless something had changed since previous years.

Michaels had managed not to make any mistakes on the icy roads, but Daniel had watched the onboards and news coverage. He'd seen the way the American was driving, taking risks at every bend as he fought to keep his championship status. Daniel understood the hunger, but he also understood the mistakes that could come from it. Given the relatively small difference in their final times, Daniel was confident he could continue to drive with the combination of skill and sense that he'd used in Sweden and still see enough wins to put him ahead in the final standings.

"Three points behind," he said with a wide grin for Frank as they approached the ceremonial finish line.

"Not bad for a driver who didn't finish last season and a co-driver who's never been at this level before," Frank replied, his grin matching Daniel's.

The smile warmed Daniel all the way through. He'd have to think on that some more later. Jean-Paul's edict continued to ring clearly in his head, but he wasn't as sure as he had been of the wisdom of the words. Despite niggling sexual tension, he had driven better than he ever had in Sweden the past three days. Granted, things were going well between them at the moment. If they'd been fighting, it would have been a different story, but they weren't, and he thought they were professional enough to keep it that way.

Driving onto the grandstand set up for this exact purpose, Daniel put the car in park and opened the door, urging Frank to get out on the other side. The emcee approached Daniel, microphone in hand. "Congratulations, Daniel," the emcee said in English, offering his hand. "Your first podium in Sweden. What made the difference this year?"

Daniel returned the handshake with a smile. "You ask easy questions this time," Daniel said with a laugh. "All credit for the drive this year goes to my new co-driver, Frank Dufour. He makes sure I do not do…." He looked over at Frank. "*Bétises*?"

"Stupid mistakes," Frank supplied with a grin.

"He makes sure I do not do stupid mistakes," Daniel said, turning back to the emcee.

"He must be one heck of a co-driver then," the emcee replied, "because your performance this rally has been impressive."

"Wait 'til you see us with no ice," Daniel said with a cocky grin. "We'll make this rally's performance look shabby."

"That will be a treat," the emcee said, shaking Daniel's hand again, all the cue Daniel needed to know the interview was over. He climbed back in the car and ceded his place to Michaels, in line behind him.

Pulling the car to the side of the road so they could hear the rest of the interviews, Daniel grinned at Frank again. "We're on our way."

Frank nodded. "There's Michaels."

Daniel grimaced and resisted the urge to roll his eyes. Michaels was an amazing driver, but he'd never given Daniel much reason to think well of him as a man. He was brash as only Americans could be and had none of the modesty, real or feigned, that the European and Asian drivers showed when they won.

"You drove a great race," the emcee said, shaking Michaels's hand.

"We came in second," Michaels said, his voice flat, "but that won't happen again. Once we're off the ice, we'll be unstoppable. All anyone will see of us for the rest of the season will be our taillights."

"That's a very confident statement," the emcee commented, clearly unprepared for Michaels's attitude.

"What an ass!" Frank muttered.

Daniel agreed wholeheartedly. "Now you see why I want the championship or at least don't want him to get it again."

"For sure," Frank agreed. "Let's go. Unless you want to see Asikainen come across."

"He deserved to win," Daniel said. "He drove the best and managed the ice in a way neither Michaels nor I did. Michaels can say what he wants. I'll be happy to shake Asikainen's hand."

Frank nodded. "I spent most of my time studying the videos of your drives so I could help us improve for the next day, but Asikainen had to manage the ice to beat your time because you drove clean, other than the one brush against the snow bank that first day."

Michaels drove off the podium and Asikainen arrived to deafening cheers from the locals who were always happy to see a Nordic driver win. The emcee switched languages so Daniel didn't understand what they were saying, but from the crowd's applause, Daniel suspected Asikainen had been his usual gracious self.

"It'll be awhile before he gets free," Daniel said as the rally committee chair brought huge magnums of champagne to Asikainen and his co-driver. "We'll find them later this evening and congratulate them. Isabelle will be getting restless, wondering what we've done with her car."

"*Her* car?" Frank joked as Daniel put the car in gear and headed back to the garage.

"You'll never convince her otherwise," Daniel said. "She rebuilt it completely to WRC specifications and her own vision. The paddle shifter certainly isn't standard gear and is something I'd never heard of before she installed it, so you know I didn't suggest it."

"I think that's as much the reason for your time improvement as me," Frank commented. "You didn't have to take your hand off the wheel to shift so you had better control of the car the entire time."

"Don't sell yourself short," Daniel insisted. "Yes, it made a difference, but having you in the car with me made more of one."

They reached the garage to the cheers of the rest of the team. Daniel smiled and accepted the claps on the back from the people who made his career possible. "Are we ready for Jordan?" he shouted.

The entire team let up a cheer.

THREE days later, back in Clermont-Ferrand, where the temperatures felt positively balmy in comparison to Sweden despite the snow on the ground, Frank stared at the mirror and tried to figure out what exactly he had agreed to when Dany had called to invite him to the café tonight. At first he'd thought it was just drinks as usual, but then Dany had said something about dinner and celebrating, and now Frank didn't know what to think. He didn't want to make this into something it wasn't, but at the same time, the invitation had the feeling of something different, something... *more*, and Frank could admit to himself that he wasn't opposed to that. He'd deny it to Dany, to Isa, to Jean-Paul and anyone else who asked, but alone in his apartment, he could close his eyes and remember the heat of Dany's back beneath his hands as he massaged the tense muscles. He hoped the plane ride home from Sweden hadn't caused more problems, but he didn't know how to ask without seeming overeager. It had been one thing during the rally when Dany had complained openly about his back hurting. Then, it had been simply a question of helping out a teammate. To offer now would imply a greater intimacy than Frank was comfortable with initiating.

He snorted in self-derision and finished getting ready. They'd run a good race. They had a few days off before they had to leave for Jordan to meet the crew and the car there for some acclimation time before the next rally started. He could enjoy dinner and drinks with a friend without it having to be anything more than that.

So why did it feel like a date?

The café was crowded as it always was on a Friday night, the regulars filling most of the tables and crowding around the bar. Frank hung back, looking around for Dany to no avail, but Jacques, the owner, caught sight of him near the door and called him over by name.

"*Eh, les mecs!*" he announced to the café in general. "Look who's here!"

Frank flushed, not expecting the cheer that went up when the regulars saw him standing next to Jacques near the bar.

"All I did was navigate," Frank demurred.

"And after last year, we all learned how important that is," Jacques insisted, "*n'est-ce pas?*"

Another cheer met Jacques's words. "Drinks on me tonight," Jacques finished, patting Frank on the back. "What can I get you?"

"A kir royal," Frank decided after a moment. "I'll probably get wine for dinner, but not until Dany gets here."

Jacques moved behind the bar, mixing the cassis and champagne and handing it to Frank. Frank sipped, finding it just the right blend of sweet and tart. "Very good," he said, tipping the glass in Jacques's direction.

Dany arrived a moment later, looking far too tempting with his hair windblown and his cheeks flushed from the cold. Frank took a big sip of his drink to cover his reaction. Fortunately the regulars at the café swamped Dany as soon as the door shut behind him, giving Frank a chance to recover his composure somewhat before Dany finally made it to his side. "I see you've been here awhile."

"Not that long," Frank said, "but Jacques stuck a drink in my hand the moment I walked in the door."

"We raced well," Dany said as if that were an explanation. "As long as we do, drinks are on the house."

"That's what he said," Frank agreed. "You should get something."

Dany chuckled, confusing Frank, but as he turned around, Jacques passed a drink across the bar. "Jacques already knows what I drink when I'm winning."

Frank touched his glass to Dany's. "Apparently we have the same taste in drinks."

"Apparently we have the same taste in a lot of things," Dany amended.

Frank wanted to ask what other tastes they shared, but he wasn't sure that was a conversation for a public place.

They sipped their drinks, waiting for a table to clear, but it appeared the patrons had settled in for the night, watching the soccer match and cheering as loudly as if they were in the stadium. "Shall we eat here at the bar?" Frank asked eventually, his stomach grumbling unhappily.

"We can," Dany said, "or we can thank Jacques and go somewhere quieter."

"I thought you wanted to celebrate with your friends," Frank said, confused.

"I do," Dany said, "but the last time I checked, you were my friend as well, and they've cheered me, and Jacques has given me my celebratory drink. I've done my duty by them and they by me."

Frank shook his head even as he laughed, his brow furrowed with puzzlement. "I don't get it. I thought this was *your* café."

"It is," Dany said, "but that doesn't mean I'm always the center of everyone's attention. If I hadn't come while we were in town, it would have been a slap in the face to my supporters, but I don't have to spend every minute we're in town sitting here. There aren't any tables available. We aren't here to watch the match. No one will care if we go elsewhere for dinner. We'll thank Jacques, shake a few hands, pat a few shoulders, so people know we're leaving and why, and then we'll go eat dinner somewhere quiet where we can actually talk."

"Do we have things to talk about?" Frank asked.

"Jordan is nothing like Sweden," Dany said as if it was the most obvious thing in the world.

"I know that," Frank said, "but I figured we'd have plenty of time to talk about it once we got to Jordan."

"Do you want another kir before we go?" Dany asked, not addressing Frank's comment. Frank shook his head. He'd already figured out that his partner heard what he wanted to hear and ignored the rest. It wouldn't hurt, he supposed, to discuss business over dinner. At least it would put an end to his sense of this being a date.

"No, I'm fine," Frank said. "If I have another one, I won't be able to drive home."

"You can always crash at my place," Dany offered. "It's just around the corner."

Frank knew exactly where it was since he'd lived there his first two weeks in France. He wasn't sure it would be a good idea to sleep there tonight, especially not if he'd had too much to drink. His tongue tended to get the better of his common sense after too much alcohol and some things were better left unsaid.

Sex and cars don't mix.

"We'll see," Frank said, draining his glass. "Dinner would be good, though. I didn't have much for lunch and I'm getting hungry."

"Let's go, then," Dany said, finishing his drink as well. He caught Jacques's attention.

"Another round?" Jacques asked.

"Not tonight," Dany said. "We wanted dinner, but we aren't going to get a table in here with the match on."

"No, probably not," Jacques agreed. "When do you leave again?"

"In about a week," Dany replied.

"Come back on a night when there isn't a match. It will be quieter then," Jacques suggested.

Dany nodded. "I didn't even think about the match when we made our plans for tonight." He offered his hand to Jacques. "Thanks for the drink. It was wonderful as always."

"My pleasure," Jacques said, shaking Frank's hand as well. "Good luck on the next rally if I don't see you before you leave."

"Thanks."

Frank followed Dany as he made the rounds of the room, shaking hands and patting shoulders exactly as he'd said. Frank felt a little superfluous in a room full of people he barely knew, but they all shook his hand as well, wishing both of them luck at the next rally. When they'd spoken to everyone Dany felt they needed to speak to, they stepped out of the overheated, smoky café onto the street.

Frank coughed slightly as the icy night air hit him, chasing away the buzz he had going. He wrapped his scarf tighter around his neck and then took another deep breath, letting the crisp air clear his head and lungs. "So where should we go for dinner?"

"Why don't we go to my place?" Dany said. "I went shopping this morning. The butcher had fresh rabbit, and I haven't had that in ages. We eat in restaurants so much while we're at the rallies. A home-cooked meal sounds really good right now."

Frank blinked a couple of times in surprise. Dany was the one who had suggested they go out tonight. And now he was suggesting they eat at his apartment? Then again, Frank had learned while he lived with Dany that the other man could cook, and fresh rabbit sounded really good. "Okay, if you're sure you don't mind cooking."

"I wouldn't have offered if I did," Dany said, starting back toward his apartment. "Besides, I plan on making you help."

Frank's stomach curled at the thought of the casual intimacy of working in the kitchen together. It was one of the reasons he'd hurried to find his own place when he'd first moved to Clermont-Ferrand. It felt too good to share Dany's space and life. It made him want things Dany wasn't offering.

Dany tossed his coat on the back of the couch when they arrived at his place, but he took Frank's and hung it neatly in the closet. "So what did you think of your first championship rally?" Dany asked as he headed into the kitchen.

Frank trailed along behind him, already feeling overwhelmed. The kitchen was small, barely enough room for both of them, but before Frank could question the wisdom of being in there at the same time, Dany handed him a sheaf of lettuce leaves. Frank took a deep breath to settle his nerves, telling himself to stop being ridiculous as he moved to the sink to wash the greens for a salad, but he couldn't shake the feeling that something was different tonight. He glanced over at Dany, trying to figure it out, only to see the other man watching him as well.

Nerves sizzling, Frank turned quickly back to what he was doing. He wasn't a great cook, but he could make a salad, and Dany had taught him how to make a French mustard vinaigrette before he moved into his own apartment, so when he finished cleaning the lettuce, he started automatically on the dressing. As he opened the cabinet and took out the red wine vinegar without even having to think about where it was or what he was doing, his stomach took another nose dive. They weren't a couple, no matter how much it felt like it at the moment.

Sex and cars don't mix.

The admonishment did nothing to offset the tension investing his body.

"Relax," Dany said from the other end of the kitchen. "We're two friends having dinner. No one can fault us for that."

Frank's face flamed. "Am I that transparent?"

Dany shook his head. "No, but it's a little hard not to feel it. We're both adults. We can behave responsibly."

Frank summoned a smile. "Sex and cars don't mix?"

"Exactly," Dany said. If his voice lacked conviction, neither of them commented on it, much to Frank's relief.

CHAPTER ELEVEN

JORDAN was as miserably hot as Sweden had been miserably cold. Frank had known it would be that way. He'd done his research, not to mention that Dany had commented several times about the heat and the grit from the desert. It hadn't prepared him for exactly how hot it was. Forty degrees Celsius. So hot he could barely breathe outside, although at least it was a dry heat rather than humid. They'd been there for two days, and he still felt like he couldn't drink enough water.

He might have dealt with it better if he had a better sense of what was going on between him and Dany. After that fraught moment at Dany's apartment, the other man had backed off suddenly, and the rest of the evening, Dany pretended like it hadn't happened. He'd kept pretending for the rest of their short stay in Clermont-Ferrand. They were on vacation, sort of, so they didn't have to report to the garage and track every day like they'd been doing since Frank moved there in September, leaving Frank at loose ends. Always before, they'd filled that free time together, kayaking, hiking, and flying ultralights when it was warmer, skiing when it got cold. Dany was as much of an adrenaline junkie as Frank was, yet another reason they were so well-matched in the car. After that night, though, Frank hadn't heard from Dany for three days, until it was time to leave for Jordan.

In the two days since they'd arrived, Dany had been his old friendly self when they were working, driving along desert roads to test the car in the extreme conditions even if they had to stay at legal speeds. Most of the time. Everything felt normal while they were driving, but the moment they got out of the car, Dany pulled back, leaving Frank off balance. He'd gotten so used to spending all his time with Dany that he hadn't really gotten to know any of the other crew besides Isabelle, which left him at loose ends now.

He'd jumped at Dany's mention of a pre-race party at one of the clubs in Amman. He hadn't expected Dany never to leave his side—that would have looked suspicious in a country where homosexuality was taboo—but he hadn't been prepared to watch Dany surrounded by women.

He almost wished he'd stayed home. He wasn't well enough known to garner the kind of attention Dany was receiving, although a few of the women had flirted with him. Nothing like the attention Dany and the other drivers were getting, though. Not that he regretted that! He couldn't appear too uninterested and yet he was totally uninterested. Fortunately Isabelle came to his rescue, sliding up next to him and slipping her arm through his.

Frank smiled at her absently, blinking a couple of times when he got a good look at her appearance. In deference to the Islamic sensibilities of the country, she wore a loose tunic that hung almost to her knees over a pair of slacks instead of her customary jeans. Her hair was down, curling around her shoulders in riotous waves usually hidden in the ponytail or chignon she wore. She'd brushed on the slightest bit of makeup, enough to highlight her eyes. If he'd been interested in women, she would have definitely hit high on his list.

"Saving me from the locals?" he murmured.

"Saving myself," she whispered back. "They don't know what to make of me. I'm part of the team, but I'm a woman. You'd think after six years, we'd be a familiar sight, but they haven't gotten over being shocked by me yet."

"You can spend all evening on my arm if you want," Frank promised.

"It's safer than where you'd like to be," Isabelle replied.

"There's nowhere I'd rather be than right here with you," Frank said, hoping the words didn't sound like quite the lie they were. He couldn't go where he wanted, and not simply because homosexuality was frowned upon in Jordan.

Sex and cars don't mix.

The hated words ran through his head like a litany as he watched Dany pull one of the women at the club onto the dance floor.

"Watch your expression," Isabelle murmured at his side. "No one else understands your reasons for looking murderous at a party."

"And you do?" Frank asked.

"My brother sees a chance at a winning season, and not just a winning season, but a championship," Isabelle explained softly. "He's had winning seasons, but he's never had a championship. He isn't going to do anything to endanger that."

"Why is everyone so convinced that a deeper relationship between us would endanger that?" Frank asked seriously. "It seems to me the better we know each other, the better we'll communicate during a race."

Isabelle shrugged, her reply forestalled by Michaels's approach. "What are you doing here?" he sneered at her. "I thought this was a party for drivers and co-drivers."

"And their dates," Frank interrupted, not liking the man's attitude. Isabelle squeezed his arm in silent warning.

"Sour grapes are so unattractive, Michaels," Isabelle said.

"Sour grapes?" Michaels repeated. "Last I checked, I beat your sorry team in Sweden."

"By a fraction of a minute," Isabelle reminded him. "On our worst surface. You're going down this season and you know it."

"Unless your lazy excuse for a brother has gotten better on gravel since last year, there's no way he'll beat me on any of those courses," Michaels retorted. "And there are still more gravel rallies than anything else."

"But he has gotten better," Isabelle said. "You saw him drive in Sweden. He's never driven like that, and that will be even more obvious once the rally starts here. He may not win every race, but he'll win enough to beat you."

"How?" Michaels scoffed.

Isabelle smiled mysteriously. "Wouldn't you like to know? Come on, Frank. There's someone I want you to meet. Someone worth knowing."

As they crossed the room, Frank said, "Is he always so obnoxious?"

"That was nicer than usual," Isabelle said, rolling her eyes. "Forget about him. I really do want to introduce you to an old friend."

Frank let her lead him across the room. He recognized Christophe Roca, Dany's former co-driver. Isabelle embraced Christophe, kissing both his cheeks before introducing Frank.

"Nice to meet you, sir," Frank said, offering his hand. "I was a fan of yours for years. What brings you to Jordan?"

Christophe laughed. "I retired here, believe it or not. It's beautiful country, and I fell in love with it when we first raced here. You and Daniel had an impressive first race a few weeks ago."

"Thank you," Frank said. "It's always a little disappointing not to win, but we were pleased with the overall results."

"You can't win them all," Christophe said, "but it looked to me like Daniel's driving was steadier than I've ever seen it, so whatever you two are doing, it's obviously working."

"We do seem to make a good team," Frank agreed, "although at the moment, he's annoying me."

"Take Frank for a walk," Isabelle told Christophe, "and explain my brother to him."

"What exactly am I supposed to explain?" Christophe said with a laugh.

Isabelle tilted her head toward where Dany was leading a woman off the dance floor. "Why that"—her scowl deepened when Dany and the woman left—"will never be a threat to him."

"Ah," Christophe said with a sage nod. "I think I see the problem. Shall we take a stroll? The temperature cools off in the evenings, and you may prefer not to have our conversation overheard."

Frank nodded, not sure what else to say. He'd gotten used to Isabelle's blunt speech, but he didn't know Christophe except by reputation. Isabelle obviously trusted him, or she wouldn't have been as blunt as she was, especially not here. He'd seen her with the mechanics from other teams. She could be cagey when she needed to be.

They found a table on the patio outside the club, taking seats side by side. Christophe pulled out a cigarette and offered one to Frank, but Frank shook his head. "Do you mind if I do?"

"No, go ahead," Frank said, grateful for the momentary delay.

When the tip of Christophe's cigarette glowed red against the darkness, he leaned back in the chair and looked at Frank speculatively. "You obviously have an impressive rapport with Daniel," the older man said slowly. "You don't need me to tell you that he's never driven like he did in Sweden."

"Jean-Paul already told us," Frank admitted. "I think he hoped to use it as a way to keep Dany under control."

"You call him Dany," Christophe said with a chuckle. "I'm impressed. He doesn't let many people call him that."

"Isabelle calls him that all the time," Frank protested.

"She does," Christophe agreed, "but she's his sister, however much he might lament that fact on occasion. She's also, if you pay attention, one of the few people who calls him that."

"I hadn't noticed," Frank admitted. "I spent so much time with her going over the mechanical aspects of the car when we first started out that I got to thinking of him that way and never thought about what anyone else called him. He hasn't said anything to me about it."

Christophe nodded his head slowly. "Isabelle seems to think you're worried about Daniel's tomcatting. Is it because he isn't focused on the race or because he isn't focused on you?"

"That's an awfully big leap," Frank replied, not comfortable admitting his feelings for Dany to a virtual stranger.

"It would be if Isabelle hadn't dragged you over to me and said what she said," Christophe agreed, "but Isabelle is not terribly subtle at the best of times. Tonight she wasn't even trying."

"So can you reassure me like she wanted?" Frank asked.

"I haven't talked to Daniel other than to say hello since he arrived tonight," Christophe said, "so I can't tell you if your interest is returned, but I can tell you that the women at events like this are a dime a dozen to him. He doesn't see them. They're there, they're on offer, and it's expected, so he trolls the room and adds to his reputation, but they don't mean anything. Nothing shakes his focus on a race, certainly not some bimbo in a bar. The bond he had with me when we were driving together, and the bond he must have with you to have driven the way he did, is far stronger than any lure they put out. He'll be back in his hotel room in a couple of hours, thinking about what needs to be done tomorrow, not about them."

"I lost my last job because I'm gay," Frank said, not entirely sure why he was telling Christophe this. "Jean-Paul knows about it, and it isn't a problem with this team, but he warned Dany away from me before I ever arrived. 'Sex and cars don't mix.' Do you think he's right?"

Christophe pondered the question for a moment before replying slowly, "Sex and cars don't mix, but you don't strike me as the fuck and run type. No one knows me like my wife. No one can read me like she can. As far as I know, there's never been a husband-wife team on the rally circuit, but I bet if there were, they'd be a seamless pair."

"So what are you saying?" Frank pressed.

"I'm saying that if you and Dany are just messing around to pass the time, then Jean-Paul's right," Christophe answered, "but if you're both serious, it might make your working relationship even stronger. Consider this, though. If you start a romantic relationship and it goes wrong, you'll probably lose your working relationship entirely. Not purposely, but can you imagine sitting in a car for hours on end with an ex, even if it's an amicable parting?"

"So are you encouraging or discouraging me?" Frank asked.

"Neither," Christophe said. "I don't know how serious your interest in Daniel is, nor do I know how seriously he returns your interest, if at all. I want Daniel to be happy. Winning will do that for him, and you've shown you have a good chance of winning a number of races this season, perhaps even the championship, although it's too soon to make any real predictions on that count. I'm also a romantic at heart. I married my first love as soon as she would have me and haven't looked back. I highly recommend the state when it comes to happiness, but relationships can be rocky at times. Keep all that in mind when you make your decision."

THE rally was almost anticlimactic in comparison, if driving at ridiculous speeds through mountainous desert roads with crazy ascents and descents could be called anticlimactic. Once again, they ran a clean race, coming in a very close second behind Michaels. Asikainen didn't even finish, retiring after a mechanical failure on the second day, leaving Michaels in first place overall with Dany and Frank only ten points behind in the championship race.

Far more interesting as far as Frank was concerned was how Christophe's predictions had played out. The night at the club, Frank had hardly seen Dany, but he was awake and at the service park even before Isabelle the next morning, and he was as focused on the race as he had been in Sweden. Whatever had transpired with the woman or women at the bar, it had no bearing on the race.

The heat had been nearly as hard to deal with as the cold in Sweden, their protective gear a hindrance in the sweltering temperatures. Dany's back hadn't seized quite as badly as in Sweden, but Frank hadn't given it the chance, either, following Dany back to his room after the shakedowns and the actual race days to massage the tense muscles. The first day, Dany had seemed surprised, though he didn't protest. After that, he didn't even seem surprised.

Frank couldn't decide what that meant, although he knew what he wanted it to mean. He wanted it to mean Dany was as eager for the moments of contact as Frank was. He wanted it to mean Dany looked to him for more than help on the rally course, but he couldn't be sure. The massages did help on the course the next day, after all, even if they meant far more than that to Frank. He could feel the closeness growing between them. Their interactions had gotten even smoother during the rally, Frank sensing the best time to give Dany the information he needed for the next section of the stage. They had started anticipating each other off the race course as well, handing each other things without the other having to ask. His parents had done the same thing, but he'd never seen that kind of familiarity outside of married couples. It made him wonder what they'd be like if they were a couple. And then it made him wonder what would happen if they couldn't make it as a couple, and each time he had that thought, he bit back the words he'd been about to say.

CHAPTER TWELVE

ELATION flooded through Daniel as the Bulgarian rally organizer gave him the signal to approach the platform for the ceremonial finish. He glanced at Frank, grinning in the seat next to him. "Ready to do this?"

Frank's grin widened. "Hell yes."

Daniel gunned the engine so the car crested the rise with a guttural roar to the cheers and shouts of the rally fans. Cutting the engine, he looked at Frank once more, nodding so they opened the doors and stepped out together. Maybe it was empty symbolism to everyone but him, but Daniel knew he wouldn't be here on the podium in Bulgaria if it weren't for Frank. He didn't want anyone thinking even for a moment that Frank should take second place to him in this celebration.

"Congratulations!" the emcee said, stepping up onto the stand next to Daniel.

"Thank you," Daniel said, conscious of his heavy accent, but determined to continue. "I couldn't have done it without my co-driver. Frank, come over here too."

Frank looked surprised as he walked around to Daniel's side of the car, but he came willingly enough. Daniel draped his arm casually over Frank's shoulders. "Don't let anyone tell you differently," Daniel said, leaning in as if telling the emcee a secret. "This is the secret to my success right here."

"You do seem to be having an outstanding season so far this year," the emcee agreed. "Third in Sweden, second in Jordan, and now first here in Bulgaria. You're driving a new car this year as well. Has that made any difference?"

"In some ways, it's harder," Daniel admitted, "because even with all the tests we did, I'm not as familiar as I was with the C4, but my sister—you know she is my lead mechanic—she is a genius. She did some things under the hood, and especially with the new paddle shifter that make this a faster car."

"It sounds like you're fortunate to have her," the emcee said.

"I'm fortunate in my whole team," Daniel said firmly. "I might be the one to go out and represent us, but they're the ones who make it possible. Anyone who says different is self-important."

The crowd cheered loudly at that.

"Your fans certainly appreciate your attitude," the emcee said. "If you're ready, then, we'll break out the champagne."

Daniel grinned. "Ready, Frank?" he asked, switching back to French.

Frank grinned and winked as they walked to the front of the car to meet the representative of the rally who brought two huge magnums of champagne. Daniel took one as Frank took the other. Shaking the bottles for maximum effect, they climbed onto the roof of the car.

Daniel looked at Frank once more to make sure he was ready before they popped the corks and sprayed the car and each other with champagne. The crowd cheered, and the rest of the team, Isabelle in the lead, came out to join them on the podium. Elated, Daniel sprayed them as well. Some of them scattered a bit, but most of them simply joined in the cheering.

"We have to celebrate tonight!" Daniel shouted to Frank over the noise of the team and the crowd. "We're going to paint the town red!"

Frank didn't try to reply, only nodding and smiling as they continued to wave to the crowd. Daniel took it as an affirmative. He'd had enough experience reading Frank's expressions that he was pretty sure he knew them all at this point. All except the one he most wanted to see.

Sex and cars don't mix.

He'd lost track of how many times he'd repeated that in his head in the six weeks since the rally in Sweden. At the end of any day they spent in the car, Frank would follow him back to his room and give him a massage. The routine had become comfortable, and Daniel was sure he'd never felt this good physically during a season as he did now. His back hardly hurt even after a full day's racing. The sensation of Frank's hands on his skin hadn't grown any less powerful for being routine. Daniel had taken to pretending to fall asleep so he wouldn't have to roll over and reveal his erection as he said goodbye. He'd thought more than once about telling Frank he didn't need the massages anymore, but that would mean giving up the little bit of intimate contact between them, and Daniel couldn't make himself do that.

He'd had delusions of fucking Frank out of his system, or at least forgetting about him for a while in someone else's arms, but that had failed spectacularly in Jordan. The woman he'd gone off with—he couldn't even remember her name—had been as beautiful as he could have asked for and more than willing to do anything he wanted, but his release had been temporary. When he'd come down from the physical high, his first thought had been to wonder what Frank would think about him having gone off this way. The answer his conscience supplied was not at all reassuring.

He'd tried telling himself he was being ridiculous, that he and Frank hadn't made any promises—they hadn't even kissed, for Christ's sake! None of that mattered, apparently, because he'd left the woman's arms and gone back to his empty bed so he'd be ready to go the next morning, the rally and Frank's good opinion more important than any fleeting pleasure he could find in her arms.

Feeling finally like they'd done their duty on the public front, Daniel hopped down from the car and waited for Frank to join him so they could return the car to the garage, get cleaned up, and go out.

"They don't do it up this big on the J-WRC," Frank said as he climbed into his seat.

"You're playing with the big boys now," Daniel said with a grin. "Come on, let's get the car back to Isabelle so we can go out."

"Where are we going?"

"Somewhere we can walk," Daniel said. "We're celebrating. Neither of us will be in any shape to drive home by the end of the night."

"Are you going to get me drunk and take advantage of me?" Frank joked.

Daniel knew he was joking. The grin, the light in his eyes, the tone of his voice all proclaimed his teasing intent, but the images evoked by the words were nearly irresistible. "Would you complain if I did?" he asked hoarsely.

A rap on the hood of the car shattered the moment. Daniel cursed under his breath as he started the car again and drove back to the garage, the silence between them tense for the first time in their friendship.

Frank disappeared the moment they reached the garage, before Daniel could catch him to confirm their plans for the evening. Daniel chafed at the questions Isabelle asked him about how the car had run and if he'd noticed anything that needed to be smoothed out before the next race in Australia in a month's time. He answered her as minimally as possible, but even so, by the time she let him go, warning him she had more questions and they'd talk again tomorrow, Frank was nowhere around.

Daniel returned to the hotel and showered quickly, changing out of his racing clothes and into a pair of slacks and sweater suitable for an evening out. Determined not to let Frank get away from him again, he hurried down the hall to Frank's room, knocking on the door.

"Just a minute!" Frank called from within.

Daniel felt everything inside him relax. He had no idea what reaction he'd get when Frank opened the door, but at least the other man was there and Daniel would get a chance to set things right between them again.

It took Frank more than a minute to answer the door, but Daniel waited patiently. When the door finally opened, Daniel summoned his best smile. "Ready to celebrate?"

"Not quite," Frank said, looking down at his bare feet, "but you can come in if you want. I'll be another few minutes at the most."

Daniel followed Frank back inside, trying not to stare at the tight, compact body in front of him. It was a little hard in the narrow entry into the hotel room.

"I asked at the reception desk on my way back in," Frank said, turning back and nearly catching Daniel staring. He dragged his eyes quickly up to Frank's face, hoping he wasn't blushing. "There's a club down the street that serves decent food as well. We can have dinner and then stay as long as we want at the bar or on the dance floor."

"Sounds great," Daniel said. "I promise not to run off and abandon you this time."

"You didn't abandon me last time," Frank said. "Isabelle kept me company and introduced me to Christophe. We had a very interesting chat."

"Did he tell you all my deep, dark secrets?" Daniel joked, trying to keep the conversation light. The thought of Christophe and Frank talking made him a little nervous, actually, because Christophe knew him better than anyone except Isabelle.

"You mean I didn't know them all already?" Frank countered. "I'm hurt."

Daniel revised his earlier thought. Maybe Frank figured up on that list of people who knew him well too. "I'm an open book."

Frank snorted in amusement, slipping on socks and shoes. "There are so many comments I could make to that, but if I do, we'll never get out of here, and I'm hungry."

Daniel spluttered in indignation as Frank stuck his wallet in his pocket and walked to the door. "Are you coming? I wasn't kidding about being hungry."

Daniel followed Frank out of the room and down the street to the club he'd mentioned. At the relatively early hour, it wasn't crowded yet, and they had no problem getting a table near the back wall where they'd have some measure of privacy. Their waiter spoke very little English and even less French, but the menu was translated into multiple languages, so with judicious pointing, they were able to place their order. The waiter returned with their drinks in short order.

Daniel raised his glass, Frank following suit. "To Bulgaria!"

"To winning!" Frank agreed.

They clinked their glasses and drank the first of many rounds.

WHEN they finally staggered back into the hotel five hours later, neither of them was walking straight, but Daniel didn't care. It gave him an excuse to bump into Frank. Repeatedly. As they climbed the stairs to their floor, Daniel gave an exaggerated groan. "My back is killing me."

Frank looked at him a little suspiciously, but they were both drunk, and it had become routine at the end of a day of racing. "The liniment is in my room," Frank slurred. "I'll get it and join you in your room. I don't want you falling asleep in my bed."

"You don't want to sleep with me?" Daniel teased, his enunciation no better than Frank's.

"I've seen you sleep," Frank said. "You take up the whole bed. There wouldn't be any room for me."

"I'd make room for you," Daniel promised, trying to keep his tone light despite the suddenly seriousness behind the words.

"Go get undressed," Frank said, pushing Daniel down the hall toward his room. "I'll be there in a minute."

Daniel let himself into his room, wishing suddenly that he hadn't drunk so much. Everything felt fuzzy, and he worried about misreading the situation because of it. He knew what he wanted, but he'd told himself he couldn't have it. Suddenly, with inhibitions lowered by alcohol, the reasons why seemed less important. He tried to summon the serious expression on Jean-Paul's face and the mantra that had kept him in line since September, but he couldn't bring either of them into focus. He stripped off his pants and sweater, lying facedown on the bed in nothing but his shorts. Frank would probably make a comment about it, but Daniel would say he didn't want to get liniment on his good trousers and was too drunk to dig out a pair of old sweats.

He didn't hear Frank come in, but he heard the door to the hotel room click shut, and then Frank's familiar weight straddled his legs, and the strong, careful hands settled on his lower back, the smell of liniment assailing his nose as Frank began to massage in silence.

Daniel lay there for several long minutes, letting Frank's hands work their magic on his stiff muscles. He'd exaggerated how badly his back ached, a ploy to land them in this exact situation, but he hadn't outright lied, and the massage felt good. Eventually, his muscles relaxed and Frank's hands had other effects on Daniel's body.

If he'd had less to drink, Daniel was sure he'd have found a way to dismiss the thought that Frank's strokes over his skin felt different tonight. Usually Daniel knew Frank was focused on easing aching muscles no matter how else the massage affected Daniel, but tonight the movement of his hands felt like a caress.

Throwing caution to the wind, Daniel rolled beneath Frank's hands. They stilled but didn't pull away, the long fingers resting on Daniel's belly, directly below his navel.

Later, Daniel couldn't have said which of them moved first, breaking the frozen tableau and the unspoken taboo. All he knew was that Frank's lips were on his, kissing him. Devouring him. He tugged on Frank's shoulders, wanting to feel the full length of the other man's body against his. When Frank finally gave in, Daniel groaned in relief and delight at the weight pressing him into the mattress.

For the first few minutes, Daniel luxuriated in the sensation of kissing and being kissed by another man. No matter what anyone said, men and women kissed differently. Even the most aggressive women usually backed down if Daniel tried to take control of their kiss, but Frank wasn't backing down, so that the kiss became a contest of wills as much as an expression of desire. Daniel had no doubt about Frank's interest. He could feel the proof of it rubbing against his own as Frank pinned him to the bed. Deciding the fight for dominance wasn't one he needed to win, Daniel relaxed into the kiss, giving Frank control of his mouth. He was more interested in other things, like getting rid of the layer of cloth between their chests.

He slid his hands down Frank's back and beneath the hem of his sweater, seeking bare skin. He kneaded the muscles of Frank's lower back in pale imitation of the wonderful massages Frank always gave him, amazed at the heat of the other man's skin. Working the sweater up, he broke the kiss long enough to pull the garment free.

To his delight, Frank dove right back into the kiss, hands on either side of Daniel's head, pinning him in place. Not that Daniel wanted to get away, although he'd eventually have to move to get supplies if this ended up where he thought it was going. Condoms and lube were quickly becoming a necessity.

His hands returned to their wandering, down Frank's back and up again, learning by touch the contours he had already studied by sight. He'd known the moment he laid eyes on Frank that there was a body beneath his clothes worthy of interest, but he was only now realizing how worthy as Frank's muscles flexed and gave beneath his hands. He thought he could spend hours doing nothing more than touching. Not tonight, though. Tonight he was too needy. This had been building for too long to end any way but fucking. They could touch and taste and explore later.

Frank tasted so good that Daniel was loath to stop kissing him long enough to fetch what they'd need. They could get off this way, he supposed, and worry about condoms and lube in the morning when they woke up. It wouldn't be quite as satisfying, but it would be better than moving now. Then Frank thrust against him hard, and Daniel changed his mind. Frottage wasn't going to cut it tonight.

Daniel broke the kiss, delighted to feel Frank trying to recapture his mouth. "Let me up for a minute," Daniel gasped as Frank attacked his neck instead. "I've got condoms and lube in the bathroom. We need them. Now."

Daniel was prepared for several reactions to his statement, from an unwillingness to let him move for even such a short time to an admonition to hurry. He didn't expect Frank to roll away from him and grab his discarded sweater. "We can't do this."

Daniel blinked a couple of times, trying to clear the mixture of alcohol and lust that had obviously addled his brains. "What are you talking about? What can't we do?"

Frank pulled the sweater over his head. "We can't fall into bed like it won't change anything. Sex and cars don't mix."

Daniel recoiled as if Frank had slapped him. "Then what the hell were we just doing?"

"Making a mistake." Frank scrubbed at his face. "We're drunk, Dany. We'll talk in the morning and figure it out, but doing this tonight… we can't."

Frank obviously had a different opinion of their capabilities than Daniel did since he was raring to go, but before he could say that or anything else to get the proceedings back on track, Frank walked out, the door swinging shut behind him with an unpleasant air of finality.

Daniel collapsed back on the bed, body aching with pent-up need and heart aching with rejection. "Fuck."

CHAPTER
THIRTEEN

DANIEL woke up the next morning with a nasty hangover and the temper to match. He was tempted to go pound on Frank's door right away and demand an explanation for the night before, but he knew if he went in his current state, they'd end up fighting instead of talking. While that might be satisfying on one level, he doubted it would get them back where they were last night before Frank's conscience or whatever it was kicked in.

Scowling at himself in the mirror, he went through his morning routine of shaving and showering. That took care of the foul taste in his mouth and most of the haggard appearance, but it didn't do much for his pounding head. He'd need coffee and food for that. Fortunately the hotel offered breakfast, so he went downstairs, pointedly ignoring Frank's closed door.

The smell of coffee greeted him as soon as he entered the hotel lobby. Pouring himself a cup, he selected a couple of croissants, all his stomach was willing to consider after last night, and took a table in a corner where he wouldn't be disturbed.

It didn't work. He'd barely taken two sips when a shadow fell across his plate.

"There's been a change of plans," Jean-Paul said unceremoniously, taking the seat across from Daniel.

"Good morning to you too," Daniel said grumpily.

"You're hungover," Jean-Paul said. "I get it, but we need to talk anyway. Frank woke me up an hour ago saying he'd gotten a call from his mother. His sister is in the hospital. They're trying to keep both her and her baby alive. He went to the airport, hoping to catch the first available flight to Canada."

Daniel's stomach turned, bile rising in his throat. "What's wrong with his sister?" he made himself ask, knowing how panicked he'd be if anything happened to Isabelle. "Did he say?"

"Complications with her pregnancy is all he said," Jean-Paul replied, "and something about trying to keep her and the baby going until the baby was far enough along for them to do an emergency C-section. He wasn't making a whole lot of sense, honestly. I sent one of the mechanics with him to the airport to make sure he got on a plane safely because I wasn't sure he could manage on his own."

"You should've gotten me," Daniel said, the previous night's tension forgotten in his worry now. "I'd have gone with him."

"I suggested it first, actually," Jean-Paul said, "but he didn't want to disturb you. I was about to insist when Pascal walked by and saw us talking. He was already up and dressed, so he volunteered to take Frank to the airport."

Daniel took a sip of his coffee, trying to buy a little time to squelch his emotions before replying. Yes, they'd had an awkward situation last night, but he still considered Frank a friend. Frank was certainly still a teammate. He thought Frank would have known that, but maybe not.

"Did he say how long he expected to stay in Canada?" Daniel asked after a minute, trying to focus on the business side of the problem and not on his sense of betrayal.

"He said he knew we had to be ready to go in Australia on April 25th," Jean-Paul said. "He knows we can't start the race without him. That's almost four weeks away. Whatever's going to happen with his sister, surely it will have happened by then."

"We'll cite a family emergency if he's absent from the promotional and preparatory work we do between now and then?" Daniel asked. "He'll be okay with that?"

"I think as long as we don't give personal details, Frank will be okay with it. On a publicity front, given the problems with Xavier and Frank's abrupt dismissal from his team two years ago, we'll want to make it clear there isn't any tension on the team," Jean-Paul said. "You put on a good show yesterday, making sure he came around while you were talking and crediting him with your improved performance. There will be questions about his absence, I'm sure, but we'll simply have to assure everyone we'll be in top form in Australia."

"I can do that," Daniel said. "After a few more cups of coffee, anyway."

"I'll deal with the press this morning," Jean-Paul promised, "but you'll have to make some kind of appearance this afternoon."

"Prepare a statement so I can see what our official line on his absence is," Daniel replied, "and I'll keep to those sentiments even if I vary the words a bit so it doesn't sound like an official line."

Jean-Paul nodded. "This is a bump in the road, not a crash. We'll be back on track in no time. Frank said he'd call in a few days when he has a better idea of what's going on. My guess is his mother wasn't much more coherent about the problems than he was this morning."

"Thanks for letting me know," Daniel said, still not sure how he felt about Frank leaving without coming to tell Daniel himself, but he couldn't let himself dwell on it. Not now. With Frank gone, all of the publicity would fall to him, and that meant putting on his best smile and doing the team proud.

"GOOD afternoon," Daniel said, taking a seat on the couch in the hotel lobby where he had agreed to meet with one of the reporters who followed the WRC. "Thank you for waiting until this afternoon for the interview. We celebrated late last night."

"Congratulations on your win," the reporter said, offering Daniel his hand. "I'd hoped your co-driver would be joining us as well."

Daniel smiled for the film crew, trying to look happy to be there and concerned for his co-driver at the same time. "Unfortunately he won't be here. He had a family emergency and has returned to Canada for a few days."

"That's going to make preparing for Australia a challenge," the reporter commented.

"We're all aware of what's at stake," Daniel replied, "but given the circumstances, we'll simply have to make the best of the situation. I can't race with any co-driver except Frank, but that doesn't mean I can't practice with a different co-driver. My sister has already offered to fill his shoes on any test runs we do until Frank can return."

"You mentioned your sister yesterday at your victory celebration," the reporter said. "Tell us a little bit about the modifications she's made to the new car."

Daniel breathed a sigh of relief, though he did his best to hide it. This was familiar. He could talk about the car all day without having to worry about the minefield of emotions currently associated with Frank and his absence. He thought he'd deflected public interest and made it clear Frank's absence was a non-issue on a professional front, but that didn't make his absence any less difficult for Daniel, given how they had parted before Frank was called home.

When they finished the interview fifteen minutes later, Daniel was drained, but he felt like he'd represented the team well, answered the questions truthfully, and avoided giving away anything he didn't want the competition or the public to know.

Like how much Frank's absence already bothered him.

"WHAT is your problem?" Isabelle demanded, cornering Daniel in the garage a week after Frank's departure. "You're acting like you have the hangover from hell, but I know you didn't go out drinking last night, so unless you sat in your apartment and got drunk alone—and if you did, then you seriously owe me an explanation—that isn't the problem."

"Leave it alone, Isa," Daniel ground out, biting back his temper. "It's none of your business."

"It is if you snap at my mechanics for no reason," Isabelle replied.

"You snap at them all the time."

"So? You don't so they aren't used to it. Everyone's walking around on tenterhooks worried about what's going to set you off next," Isabelle protested. "They don't dare call you on it, but I'm not some random mechanic. I'm your sister. Now give. What's going on?"

"It's been a week and we haven't heard from Frank," Daniel said after another moment spent glaring at his irritating sister.

"And we still have another two and a half weeks until we have to be ready to race in Australia," Isabelle reminded him. "If things are bad, he might not have found time to call yet."

"He could at least let us know he made it to Canada safely," Daniel said, knowing Isabelle was right. There wasn't anything rational about his feelings, though. He missed Frank. However much he might not want to admit it, he'd grown used to the other man's company. He scoffed at himself silently. He'd done far more than grow used to Frank's company. He'd started falling for Frank, and that was far more dangerous.

"Give it another few days," Isabelle counseled, "and if we haven't heard from him, we can call him and ask how his sister's doing. You know him better than I do, but I got the impression he was pretty close with his family. If she's in as bad shape as Jean-Paul seemed to think she was, he probably isn't thinking about anything but her right now."

Daniel opened his mouth to protest, but she shook her head. "He doesn't need to be thinking about anything but her right now. In another two weeks, yes, he has to think about us and weigh his responsibility to his family against his responsibility to us, but that's still two weeks off. We'll call and check on him in a few days as concerned friends. We will not ask him when he's coming back. He doesn't need us to remind him of his job. He needs us to share his worry for his sister."

"I don't deal well with uncertainty," Daniel grumbled.

Isabelle laughed. "Tell me something I don't know." Letting him go, she stepped back and grabbed his helmet from the bench next to them. "Let's go for a drive. You'll feel better for it."

Daniel caught the helmet. "Where are we going?"

"Anywhere you want," Isabelle replied. "No pace notes. No stop watches. Just driving."

"Then why do we need helmets?"

"Because I know how you drive when you're upset," Isabelle said, "and I'm not taking any chances with my big brother."

THE drive started off well enough, even on unfamiliar roads. With no pace notes and no closed course, Daniel didn't push the speed limit, but he also didn't slow down for curves the way most drivers would. He trusted his control and the car's abilities that much, even in normal driving conditions.

"You should go out tonight," Isabelle said, her voice coming through the headset in his helmet. "You're tense. You need to relax."

"Getting drunk isn't going to help me relax," Daniel said.

"Getting laid might," Isabelle countered.

Daniel frowned, though he knew she couldn't see it with the helmet covering his face. "It might, but not tonight."

"Why not?" Isabelle asked. "It's always worked before."

It *had* always worked before, but now Daniel wasn't interested in getting laid. He was interested in getting Frank, and Frank was in Canada and wasn't calling. "Because I don't feel like it," he snapped.

"There's no need to take that tone," Isabelle scolded. "It was a perfectly valid question given the way you've always dealt with stress in the past."

Daniel took a deep breath and resisted the urge to tell her where she could take her familiarity and her advice and everything else. He wasn't angry at Isabelle. He wasn't even really angry at Frank. Isabelle was right about that much. Frank needed to focus on his sister and his family and the duty that had dragged him home. If their situations were reversed, Daniel would be at Isabelle's bedside every moment the hospital would let him stay there. It was the timing that frustrated him more than anything else. If it had happened between Jordan and Bulgaria, Daniel would have been worried about Frank, a little anxious that he make it back on time, but he wouldn't be fidgeting in his seat wondering about their personal relationship. If it happened even a day later, he and Frank would have talked, and Daniel would know where they stood. He wouldn't miss Frank any less because of it, but at least he'd *know*. It was the not knowing that was driving him a little crazier with each passing day.

Cursing under his breath as he nearly misjudged a curve, Daniel ordered his thoughts back on the road. They might not be racing, but a wreck was a wreck, and they didn't need more problems.

"*ÂLLO?*"

Frank's voice sounded so sleepy that Daniel redid the math in his head to make sure he hadn't miscalculated the time difference. No, it was after noon in Quebec.

"Hi, Frank. It's Dany. We hadn't heard from you, and I wanted to check on your sister."

"They delivered the baby at four this morning," Frank said, yawning. "She was only at thirty-two weeks, but they said it was either that or lose both of them."

"Then I've caught you at a bad time," Daniel said. "I'm sorry. I tried to call when I thought for sure you'd be awake."

"It's all right," Frank replied. "You couldn't have known. I'm sorry I didn't call sooner, but it's been touch and go the whole time and, well, given the way I left…."

"We'll talk about that when you get back," Daniel said quickly, not wanting to get into their last encounter over the phone. "It's waited this long. Another week and a half won't hurt."

"I hope I'll be able to leave before then," Frank said, another yawn audible through the phone. "Nadine's problems were caused by the pregnancy. Now that the baby's born, she should stabilize quickly, so it's more a question of how Pauline does. She was born awfully early."

"Yeah," Daniel said. He knew nothing about babies, but even he knew that the earlier they were born, the more chances there were for health problems. "Keep us in the loop, will you? I know we haven't met your family, but, well, we think of you as one of our family now, okay?"

"Thanks," Frank said, yawning a third time.

Daniel sighed. "Get some sleep and call when you're more awake. You aren't even going to remember this conversation."

"I'll remember," Frank promised. "Talk to you soon."

"Sleep well."

Daniel hung up the phone and stared at it blankly, not sure how to interpret the conversation. Most of it was straightforward. He could give everyone the good news that Frank's sister had her baby and was doing better, that the baby was alive and fighting to stay that way. The thorny part was the few words that dealt with them. He snorted. *Them.* Like there was a them. They were a team, but beyond that, they'd shared one aborted encounter. An incredibly erotic encounter, but still only one, and not even a complete one.

He sighed. He didn't want to have this conversation over the phone. He wasn't sure he wanted to have the conversation at all, but if they had to have it, he wanted to see Frank's face as they talked. He needed that or he'd lose his nerve completely.

He called Jean-Paul and gave him the update and then he called Isabelle.

"But that's good news," Isabelle said when he'd finished the rundown of what Frank had said. "Why do you sound so down?"

"I dunno," Daniel said. "I guess I just miss him."

Isabelle didn't say anything for so long that Daniel almost asked if she was still there. "You really like him, don't you?"

"Of course I really like him," Daniel said. "Have you seen the way I drive since he got here?"

"That isn't what I meant," Isabelle insisted. "It doesn't have anything to do with driving. You drove well with Christophe, but I didn't see you hanging out with him on your days off. I didn't see you sulking at home rather than going out in the evenings when he was out of town for something."

"Different interests," Daniel reminded her, "not to mention he's quite a bit older than me."

"So you and Frank have the same interests?"

"Sure, we went kayaking and skiing and—"

"And he likes men too," Isabelle interrupted.

Daniel flushed, glad she wasn't there to see his face. "What's that got to do with anything?"

"You always get defensive when I'm right," Isabelle said. "Good for you. You deserve to be happy with someone."

"It's not that simple, Isa," Daniel said. "We have to work together."

"So? Don't make him mad at you. Then you can work together fine," she replied. "I can't even imagine what you'd be like as a team if you were together too."

"Don't set us up for happily ever after yet, Isa, please," Daniel said. "And don't say anything to anyone else. Things are complicated at the moment and he's in Canada and I don't know what will happen when he gets back."

"I won't say anything," Isabelle promised, "but one way or another, you have to work things out with him. Friends or lovers, that's up to you, but you can't leave things unresolved. You can't put the team at risk."

"I know," Daniel assured her. "Jean-Paul made sure I knew it before Frank ever signed a contract. It was easy when it was just attraction, but now...."

"Now?" Isabelle prompted.

"Now I think it could be something more."

CHAPTER
FOURTEEN

DANIEL knew Frank was jetlagged. He'd flown into Australia too, several days ago, so he'd have time to adjust to the huge time difference before the race started. Frank had arrived last night, barely in time to meet the deadline for officially entering the rally. Frank had been asleep on his feet when he got off the plane, and Daniel wasn't sure he was any better now.

"Hey, you okay over there?" he asked when he realized Frank's pen had stopped moving despite the fact that Daniel was still dictating the pace notes as they drove recce on the sixth stage of the rally.

"What?" Frank said, blinking suddenly and jerking slightly.

"Are you okay?" Daniel repeated. "You looked like you were falling asleep."

"I'm fine," Frank said, scrubbing at his face.

Daniel slowed the car. "Read your notes back to me. I don't want to miss anything because you got in at the last minute."

"You know why I wasn't here earlier," Frank snapped. "Pauline is still in critical condition and we nearly lost her three days ago when I was first planning on leaving. Forgive me if I delayed another day to make sure my niece lived."

"I know why you didn't back sooner, but we still have a race to prepare for," Daniel replied slowly, trying to rein in his temper. "Read your notes back."

"Fine," Frank said with a huff, moving back up several lines and reading them out to Daniel. "There. Satisfied now?"

"You missed the last two bends," Daniel ground out. "Look, I know you're exhausted and I know you were gone for a reason, but we can't afford that kind of mistake. If I hadn't caught it, I'd have been racing blind. That's the kind of shit Xavier pulled, the kind of shit that got him fired."

"Are you threatening my job?" Frank asked.

"We don't have time to talk about this now," Daniel said. "We have to finish the recce before they close the course. Just stay awake, okay?"

Frank repeated each note back to Daniel for the rest of the scouting drive, his voice snippier with each comment. Daniel was tempted to say he'd proven his point except that he didn't completely trust Frank to stay awake and this way he knew Frank was paying attention.

They hadn't had time to talk about the night in Bulgaria, either, but this was hardly the right time for it. Maybe tonight, if Frank seemed at all amenable to conversation. A sideways glance revealed a tense frown on Frank's face.

Maybe tomorrow would be better.

DANIEL hoped to catch Frank before breakfast the next morning, but by the time he reached Frank's room, Frank had already left. Daniel found him in the garage, talking with Isabelle, but by then the rest of the crew had gathered as well, leaving them no chance to talk privately.

Daniel could feel the tension between them like a weight in his stomach as they waited their turn for the shakedown run. He wanted to say something, but this was hardly the moment, when he needed to concentrate on the road in front of them. At least Frank looked more awake this morning than he had the day before. The morning would be busy, but he hoped they'd get a break that afternoon before the next round of publicity. Maybe they could talk then.

They pulled up to the starting line for the shakedown run, the clock counting down the seconds until they could start.

"From Main Control 1, one hundred fifty meters straight to right, s2."

Frank's voice should have been reassuring, but the tension between them carried over to his tone, the words clipped instead of his usual relaxed drawl, like he was trying to keep everything inside. The mood infected Daniel as well, his shoulders tightening as he hit the accelerator when the clock turned to zero. It was a decent start, but not their best, the short distance to the first turn keeping him from hitting maximum speed. Daniel thought he'd judged it decently, though, working through the gears, making sure everything was functioning the way it was supposed to.

They fell back on their usual rhythm except Daniel could never quite relax into Frank's directions, the memory of him missing two cues the day before too strong for him to trust the way he always had before.

They rounded a tight bend at a slightly slower speed than usual, but the gravel shifted beneath the tires, and the car spun out of Daniel's control. It didn't flip, much to his relief, but he was sure the undercarriage took a beating as they went skidding over brush.

"Fuck," Daniel muttered when the car came to a halt. He switched to reverse, the wheels spinning as he tried to get the car back on the road. The sand simply shifted beneath the tires. "You're going to have to push," he told Frank.

Frank nodded and unbuckled his safety harness, climbing out and moving in front of the car. On Daniel's signal they tried again, finally getting the car moving. Daniel knew he should wait for Frank, but he was afraid if he stopped again before he got back on the road, they'd be stuck a second time. Even with the helmet on, he could read the scowl on Frank's face, but he didn't hit the brakes until he felt tarmac beneath the tires again.

A few moments later, Frank climbed back in and fastened the safety gear. "Thanks for waiting," he muttered.

"That entire section was the same as where we got stuck," Daniel snapped. "If I'd stopped to let you back in, you'd have had to get out and push again. I'm not going to drive off and leave you. I need you to read the pace notes."

"Yeah, that's all I'm good for, isn't it?" Frank grumbled.

Daniel opened his mouth to respond, but his good sense kicked in before he could point out that Frank was the one who'd pulled away, not Daniel.

"We are not having this conversation in the car in the middle of a shakedown," Daniel said, heading down the road again. "Keep reading the pace notes."

They made it through the rest of the run with no more mishaps, but Daniel knew their time had suffered, not just from the spin out but because he wasn't driving the way he'd done in the three previous races with Frank at his side. Maybe Jean-Paul was right. If one aborted encounter messed up their working relationship this badly, maybe it wasn't worth the risk to try for more.

"What happened?" Isabelle demanded the moment they crossed the finish line of the course. "What made you lose control like that? Did something mess up in the car?"

"The car was fine," Daniel ground out. "I misjudged the bend and the gravel on the shoulder caught the tires. You'll want to make sure I didn't jar anything loose when we went into the bushes. That underbrush was pretty thick."

Isabelle frowned. "That wasn't even a difficult bend. Did Frank not give you the pace notes correctly?"

"I don't know," Daniel snapped. "He nearly fell asleep during the recce yesterday."

"Get your head out of your ass," she said, smacking Daniel's shoulder hard. "I don't know what your problem is, but you need to talk to him and work it out. I told you before, it doesn't matter what you agree to between you, but you can't leave things undecided."

"How do you know things are undecided?" Daniel asked defensively.

"Because you drove today like you did with Xavier, like you were afraid to trust your co-driver," Isabelle replied. "Which means you don't know what he is to you right now."

She was too damn perceptive, he thought with a scowl. "Fine. Have it your way."

"Daniel Leroux, get your sorry ass in this office now!"

Daniel flinched. "I guess you aren't the only one in the mood to yell at me."

"After the way you drove, do you blame me?" Isabelle shot back. "See what he wants and then talk to Frank. I won't be responsible for my actions if you don't."

Daniel suspected he'd have far more problems than his sister's ire if he couldn't get things settled with Frank, but he had to deal with Jean-Paul first.

He walked into the office to find Frank already sitting there looking like a schoolboy in the principal's office for fighting. It gave Daniel a perverse sense of pleasure to know that whatever dressing down he was about to get, Frank would be part of it too. This was not solely his fault.

He took a seat next to Frank, his jaw set as he waited to see what Jean-Paul would say.

"What happened out there today?" Jean-Paul demanded. "You didn't drive that way together when you didn't know each other, so don't bother telling me it's because you've spent a month apart."

"I misjudged a curve," Daniel said shortly. "It happens. Even with experienced drivers and teams. You see it at every rally. Someone spins out or flips over."

"Accidents happen," Jean-Paul agreed, "but that's not what I'm talking about. You drove like you weren't completely sure what was coming up next. So either Frank forgot the pace notes or something else is going on."

"We're out of sync, is all," Daniel said. "We haven't seen each other and have barely talked in almost a month. We'll have it together by race time."

Jean-Paul's face tightened like he had more to say, but he refrained, staring at them one at a time, his gaze piercing. "One bad race wouldn't be enough to lose sponsors, but after last year, we can't afford to have problems very often. Whatever the issue is between you, get it resolved." He stared fixedly at Daniel for a minute. "You remember what I told you, don't you?"

"Yes," Daniel said. "We aren't sleeping together if that's what you're worried about."

Daniel saw Frank turn his head sharply, but he kept his eyes focused on Jean-Paul. He hadn't lied. They hadn't slept together in

Bulgaria, even if Daniel had wanted to at the time. Now he wasn't sure what he wanted.

"Get out of here, both of you," Jean-Paul said, shaking his head in exasperation. "And I expect to see the team that won in Bulgaria tomorrow when the rally actually starts."

"You will," Frank said, speaking for the first time since Daniel had come into the office.

Daniel's eyes narrowed as he followed Frank out of the office.

"We should find somewhere to—"

"We should go back to our rooms and get a good night's sleep," Frank interrupted. "The race doesn't start until four tomorrow. We can go over the pace notes in the morning so everything will be fresh in your head before we start. Michaels will go first, but we won't be far behind him. Can I get a ride back to the hotel? I'm still not completely recovered from the trip and I want to be on my toes tomorrow."

Daniel scowled, but he nodded. As they approached the rental car they had while they were in Australia, Isabelle appeared from the garage. "Oh, good, you can give me a ride back to the hotel too," she said, climbing in the back seat. "I need a shower."

"How's the car?" Daniel asked.

"You scraped the paint up nicely, but you didn't damage anything important," Isabelle said as they drove off. "I expect you to keep it that way."

"I'll do my best," Daniel promised.

"Both of you," Isabelle prodded, nudging Frank's shoulder.

"I'll do my best," Frank parroted, his voice sounding tired.

Daniel looked at him at concern, but Frank's eyes were fixed out the window on the passing scenery.

They arrived at the hotel and Frank did his best imitation of a disappearing act, but Isabelle was faster, catching his arm before he could make a run for it. He looked at her in surprise, but she said nothing, grabbing Daniel's arm as well and propelling both of them into the hotel. "You two are acting like idiots," she said when she reached the floor where the entire team had their rooms. "Everyone else is at the garage still, even Jean-Paul. Give me your key, Dany."

Daniel pulled his arm free of her grasp so he could fish the room key out of his pocket. Isabelle opened his door and pushed them both inside. "Personally I think it would solve all our problems if you two would quit fighting it and fuck each other silly, but that's not my choice to make. Neither of you is coming out of this room until you've cleared the air and decided what you want your relationship to be. I'll be outside, so don't think you can wait a few minutes and leave without me knowing it. I don't know what went wrong, but fix it."

She swept back out of the room, leaving Daniel and Frank staring after her in mute consternation.

"Did you tell her?" Frank said after a moment.

"I didn't have to," Daniel said, trying not to let the accusation raise his hackles. "She doesn't know the details, but she figured out that something was going on while you were gone."

"How?" Frank asked.

"Probably the fact that I stopped going out to clubs," Daniel admitted.

"Why would you do that?" Frank asked, his voice softer now.

Daniel took a deep breath and turned to face his co-driver, sitting in the chair by the window. "Because there wasn't anyone in the clubs I cared to spend time with," he said slowly. "You were in Canada."

Even with the distance between them, Daniel could see Frank's Adam's apple working as he swallowed a couple of times. "I… I don't know what to say."

Daniel's face fell. "You either tell me you're interested in me or you tell me to go to hell," he replied, trying to keep the hurt out of his voice.

"What about Jean-Paul's lecture?" Frank asked. "Sex and cars don't mix, remember?"

"I don't know if I believe that anymore," Daniel replied. "I mean, yeah, we'd have to be careful not to pick a fight with each other right before a race or we'll end up with bad times like we had today, but Jean-Paul gave me that lecture assuming I'd just want to fuck around and then move on. He's right about that, but I'm not so sure he's right about the rest."

"So what are you saying?" Frank asked. "That you want to give an actual relationship a try?"

"I know it's a risk," Daniel admitted, "but we're already a hell of a team. I enjoy the time we spend together away from racing as well. I thought about going out while you were gone, but another meaningless encounter didn't hold any appeal anymore. I don't know what the future holds, but I think we could have something really good together. And maybe the night before a rally starts is the wrong time to find out, but you were gone. I'm not criticizing you. If our situations had been reversed, I'd have left, too, but you have to admit the timing sucked."

Frank chuckled softly. "Yeah, I suppose it couldn't have been much worse unless the phone rang while I was still in your room in Bulgaria."

"That would almost have been easier," Daniel admitted. "Then you'd have left for family reasons rather than just walking out on me like you didn't want me."

That brought Frank to his feet and across to the foot of the bed where Daniel sat. "Don't think that," he said, sitting down next to Daniel. "We were drunk, and I was afraid you hadn't thought through what we were doing. I was afraid you'd regret it in the morning and that would mess things up between us. If my mother hadn't called, I would have come back to talk to you after I recovered from my hangover."

Daniel took a deep breath and tried to push aside the month's separation and the past two days of tension. "What would you have said?"

"I would have asked you if you had thought about the possible consequences of us sleeping together," Frank replied.

"I'm not sure I had that night," Daniel replied honestly, "but I have since then. If we were just fucking around, maybe it would be a bad idea, but I don't think it is if we're really trying to make a go of it as a couple."

"That would have been my next question," Frank said. "I would have asked what you wanted from me."

Daniel grinned, his cockiness returning along with his confidence. "Everything I can get."

Frank laughed, the sound so at odds with the tension that had led up to the moment that it startled Daniel for a moment before he joined in. Leaning forward, he captured Frank's lips with his own, stopping the sound of laughter with a kiss.

Frank leaned into the embrace immediately, his tongue tangling with Daniel's in an erotic dance that left both of them panting by the time they parted.

"Should we go tell Isabelle she got her wish?" Frank said after a moment, his eyes dancing.

Daniel grinned. "She hasn't gotten it yet."

"Do you really want her sitting outside listening while she does?" Frank countered.

"You really think telling her we've worked things out will make her go away?" Daniel said with a laugh. "You obviously don't know my sister very well. She'd press her ear to the door so she could get blackmail material."

"So what do we do?"

"We tell her she got her wish and we go to dinner," Daniel said, "without the alcohol this time since we have to race tomorrow. She won't know when we get back so she won't be able to listen in."

Frank's smile widened. "I like the way your mind works."

"I've had years to learn how to defend myself against her," Daniel said as his stomach growled. "Besides, we really do need to eat."

"Let's go," Frank said, rising and pulling Daniel to his feet. "The sooner we take care of your stomach, the sooner we can take care of other things."

CHAPTER FIFTEEN

DANIEL and Frank snuck back into the hotel after dinner, not wanting Isabelle to intercept them or anyone else to waylay them. Jean-Paul would be happy to see them laughing and smiling together, but he would want explanations, and that would take time. Time Daniel would far rather spend in bed with Frank. Fortunately it was a sentiment Frank seemed to share as they peeked down the hotel hallway to make sure no one was there before racing for Daniel's room.

The moment the door closed behind them, Frank pushed Daniel against the wall, kissing him wildly. "I thought about this while I was in Canada, at night when I could barely sleep for worrying about my sister. I'd close my eyes and remember kissing you and wonder if I'd ever get the chance again given how I left."

"I was only angry until Jean-Paul explained why you left," Daniel assured him. "Once I understood that, I missed you, I wanted to know what had happened between us, but I wasn't angry anymore."

"I missed you too," Frank said, his lips sliding across Daniel's cheek and down his neck, sending the most delicious shivers down Daniel's spine.

Feeling selfish for not returning any of the pleasure Frank was lavishing on him, Daniel slid his arms beneath the hem of Frank's shirt, seeking bare skin. Frank kissed him hard one more time before pulling back and starting to strip off his shirt. He paused with the garment halfway over his head, giving Daniel a fantastic view of his sculpted abs and chest. "Do you still have supplies?" he asked. "If I have to go to my room to get them, I shouldn't get undressed just yet."

"Get undressed," Daniel said, his grin wide as he traced the line of muscle that bisected Frank's stomach. "I'll get the supplies."

Daniel rummaged through his toiletries kit, pulling out a fresh tube of lube and a strip of condoms. Carrying them back into the main room, he stopped to stare at the vision in his bed. Frank had stripped down to his boxers, his body as hard and muscled as Daniel had imagined it would be based on the few glimpses and gropes he'd had until now. His mouth watered as he took a moment to imagine getting his hands and lips on all that soft, hair-dusted skin. He appreciated a woman's smoothness and curves, but when he was with a man, he wanted hard muscle and the rasp of chest hair, even facial hair, to remind him of his lover's gender. Frank's five o'clock shadow darkened his cheeks and a triangle of chest hair narrowed to a thin treasure trail that pointed its way south to Daniel's ultimate destination.

"God, you're beautiful."

To Daniel's surprise, Frank flushed and squirmed uncomfortably on the bed at the compliment. "And you're overdressed."

Daniel tossed the supplies on the bedside table and stripped down to his underwear, climbing on the bed and crawling up over Frank's reclining form. "Why don't you want me to compliment you?"

Frank shrugged and looked away, but Daniel caught his chin and guided his gaze back. "You don't have to answer me, but don't hide from me." He let his weight settle on top of Frank, pressing their bodies—and their erections—together. "It's hardly a secret that I find you attractive."

"I haven't had a lot of relationships," Frank admitted. "It's easier to be discreet when it's a random one-night stand than when you have a long-term lover who expects to do things with you and be seen with you."

"That's certainly true," Daniel agreed, "but nobody will even blink at seeing us together. We have a built-in excuse if we ever feel like we need to use it."

"Are you saying we should come out on the circuit?" Frank asked in surprise.

Daniel shrugged. "Not right away, necessarily. But if things really work between us, if we decide to make a go of it, then yes, I think we should. It's a little too soon to be talking about a PACS or going to Amsterdam to get married or anything like that, but if we end up at that point, I wouldn't want to hide it any more than I would want to hide it if I fell in love with a woman and got married."

Frank's arms tightened around Daniel's shoulders. "You have no idea how much it means to me to hear you say that," he said, pulling Daniel's head down for a kiss. "After what happened with my last driver and team, a part of me worried we'd have to keep hiding no matter what. I know you said Jean-Paul knew I was gay when he hired me, but that didn't mean he wanted it made public."

"I think we'd have to talk with him about when and how we'd make it public," Daniel said, "but that's a worry for later, when we're ready to make a commitment that's a matter of public record. It's nobody's business but ours if we're sleeping together."

Frank bucked his hips beneath Daniel, dislodging him and rolling him to his back. "Speaking of which," Frank said with a grin, "I've wanted to get you naked for months."

"Months?" Daniel asked in surprise, lifting his hips as Frank tugged on his underwear.

"Months," Frank confirmed, tossing Daniel's shorts to the floor.

"And now that you have me that way, what are you going to do to me?" Daniel teased.

"Fuck you so hard you can't walk tomorrow."

Desire curled hard in Daniel's gut. He didn't bottom very often, but he would do so now and gladly.

"As long as I get the chance to return the favor later," Daniel replied. "I'm an equal opportunity lover."

"Later," Frank agreed, his voice catching. Daniel wondered at that but let it go. They could discuss it when they weren't naked—or nearly so in Frank's case—and horny. Frank's hands started exploring, and all desire for conversation disappeared.

It felt good to be touched. It felt even better to be touched with affection as well as desire. It had been too long since sex had been more than a way to scratch an itch, a temporary release to get through a night or a race. Daniel hadn't tried for more than that because who would willingly put up with his crazy schedule?

He had the answer now. Frank would because Frank's schedule matched his. He didn't have to worry about Frank getting bored or impatient or angry because Daniel was out of town again.

Frank's hand circled Daniel's cock, and all thoughts flew out of his head except for one. Frank was finally touching him without holding back. He bucked up into the caress, eager for it to continue. After the past month's uncertainty, it wouldn't take long for him to come if Frank continued, but it felt too good to tell him to stop.

Frank's hand was warm in the cool room, the contrast adding another layer of sensation to the ones already assailing him. He should have been embarrassed at how hard he was already, his cock dripping all over Frank's hand, but Frank was touching him as Daniel had been dreaming about for months. He just hadn't thought anything could come of it until after their win in Bulgaria, and then Frank was gone.

Daniel caught Frank's hand and reached for the lube. "If you're going to fuck me, now's the time," he said, "because if you keep that up, I'm going to come."

"I could get you worked up again."

Daniel shook his head. "I get too sensitive after I come. It hurts to be touched for a while."

Frank's hand released Daniel's cock, giving him a moment to catch his breath and shore up his control. "We can't have that," Frank said with a grin, coating his fingers and warming the lube. "Roll over so I'm not tempted to tease you."

Daniel groaned at the thought of his cock pressed against the mattress, but Frank moved a pillow under his hips, lifting him enough that his erection wasn't caught uncomfortably between his body and the bed. The position highlighted his vulnerability, especially when Frank urged him to spread his legs and climbed between them. Daniel pushed up on his elbow, looking back over his shoulder at Frank, but Frank urged him down onto the bed with a gentle push. "Relax and let me make you feel good."

Daniel did his best to comply with Frank's request, but he was not used to being in the passenger seat. He was used to being the one in control, and giving that up now was harder than he'd expected, even with someone he trusted as much as he trusted Frank.

Then Frank's fingers teased around Daniel's entrance, and he remembered how good it could feel. He shivered and relaxed on the bed, spreading his legs a little wider to give Frank better access to his body. He moaned softly when Frank's fingers kept teasing rather than penetrating, but Frank simply ran a soothing hand down Daniel's back and kept on with what he was doing.

The teasing fingers ghosted over Daniel's hole, his perineum, over his balls and back up again, never lingering long enough to push Daniel to the point of coming, but enough to have him writhing on the bed in search of more contact. Finally, unexpectedly, Frank's fingers penetrated, finding his prostate unerringly and pressing hard. Daniel let out a hoarse shout, his knuckles going white as he fisted his hands in the sheets to keep from coming on the spot. "*Putain*, Frank!" he cursed.

"You don't want me to stop, do you?" Frank teased.

"Don't you dare!" Daniel replied. "I want you to hurry."

"No patience," Frank scolded playfully. "Maybe I should teach you some."

Daniel rolled to his back again, dislodging Frank's fingers. "You can try, but you'll end up with my cock up your ass instead. Fuck me already."

Frank looked like he wanted to continue the teasing, but Daniel grabbed the condoms and tore one open, rolling it onto Frank's erection. "Now," Daniel said firmly, lying back and spreading his legs in offering.

To Daniel's relief, that seemed to break Frank's reserve. He covered Daniel immediately, lifting his hips enough that his cock nudged Daniel's entrance. Consciously Daniel relaxed his guardian muscle, hissing slightly at the burn, but he relished even the hint of pain because it meant Frank was inside him finally. The pain would fade quickly, leaving nothing but delicious fullness.

Frank took his time with that first thrust, much to Daniel's relief since it had been several years since he'd last let anyone inside him. Finally, he rocked his way completely into Daniel's stretching body, his balls brushing Daniel's ass.

"Damn, that feels good," Daniel gasped, squirming beneath Frank to adjust the angle of penetration. "It's been awhile."

Frank grunted in reply, beginning to move more forcefully. "*Ça va?*" he asked after a moment.

"*Ouais*," Daniel drawled as he pushed up against Frank's downward thrusts. He was more than "all right" at the moment, but he was too far gone to be any more eloquent in his praise. He wrapped his legs around Frank's hips and held on for the ride.

It wouldn't have taken much to trigger Daniel's orgasm, as on edge as he had been since Frank left, but Frank didn't seem to be in any rush, his movements forceful but controlled, designed to keep Daniel on the cusp of release without actually making him climax. Daniel shivered and undulated beneath Frank, trying to speed things up, but Frank stilled his hips with a tender touch.

"Don't rush," Frank whispered, his lips brushing across Daniel's gently. "This isn't a race with the prize given to the one with the fastest time. Making love should be savored."

"We can savor it next time," Daniel said. "I need to come."

Frank shook his head. "You need to relax and let me drive. I promise it'll be worth it."

Daniel would have sulked if Frank hadn't aimed a particularly powerful thrust straight for his prostate. His words of protest turned into a gasp instead. Then Frank's lips covered his again, and Daniel gave up trying to control their interactions. The moment he gave in, Frank increased the pace, hitting Daniel's prostate more consistently and with greater force.

Daniel's back arched as he strove for more contact. Frank gave it to him, pressing into him so that his stomach rubbed against Daniel's cock, providing glorious friction on his neglected erection.

He could feel his climax building at the base of his spine, bubbling outward with a force he wouldn't be able to deny for long. Every jab of Frank's cock over his gland added to the need to come until he was mewling into Frank's mouth, begging wordlessly for release. Frank worked a hand between their straining bodies, closing it around Daniel's cock. The sudden stimulation pushed Daniel over the edge, his shaft twitching hard as it disgorged its load all over Frank's hand and their chests.

The moment Frank felt Daniel's climax, he released his control, pounding into Daniel as he strove for his own release. Daniel gasped as Frank's hips stuttered against him. For a moment, they hung there, a frozen tableau of passion. Then Frank rolled to the side, disposing of the condom. He swiped his discarded shorts across Daniel's belly, enough to get off the worst of the stickiness, although Daniel would need a shower in the morning. He started to pull Daniel back into an embrace, but he stopped, his hand hovering an inch from Daniel's body.

"Will it bother you to spoon together for a while before I go back to my room?"

Daniel pulled Frank's arm down and around him, turning onto his side so he could push back against his lover, bringing their bodies into full contact. "You can hold me all night long if you want," he replied. "That contact won't hurt. It would only hurt if you were stroking my cock or trying to get me worked up again right away."

"Good," Frank said, pressing a kiss to the nape of Daniel's neck, his breath tickling the fine hairs. "I've always been a cuddler. I miss that most of all when I pick somebody up in a bar."

"No more random hookups," Daniel said, looking back over his shoulder at Frank. "If we're going to give this a try, we're going to do it right."

Frank's arm tightened around Daniel's chest. "I wouldn't have it any other way," he replied. "It was an observation about another advantage of this new side of our relationship, that's all."

Mollified, Daniel relaxed into Frank's embrace again. "Isabelle's going to be insufferable."

"No, she won't be," Frank said.

"Why do you say that?" Daniel asked. "She's always insufferable."

"I don't know what she was like while I was gone," Frank admitted, "but she'd backed off some before I left. As for why she won't be insufferable now, I'll ask her not to say anything around the rest of the team until we're ready to make our relationship more public. She may make a few comments in private, but she's your sister. She's entitled."

Daniel scowled slightly but let it go. If Frank could keep Isabelle off their backs in front of the rest of the team, it would already be a huge improvement over her usual habit of discussing his conquests volubly in the garage the next day. Then again, Frank wasn't a conquest so maybe she'd be willing to practice some discretion where they were concerned. He could hope so, anyway.

Pulling away for a moment, he checked the alarm and switched off the lamp.

"I should get up," Frank mumbled from behind Daniel.

Daniel tugged Frank's arm back around him. "You should go to sleep. You can get up in the morning."

Frank chuckled sleepily, snuggling closer. Daniel smiled and closed his eyes. He could get used to this.

CHAPTER SIXTEEN

"THIS makes two podiums in a row," the emcee said when Daniel stepped out of his car, Frank on the opposite side, at the end of the rally three days later. The afternoon thunderstorms that had plagued Coffs Coast during the rally had not materialized yet that day, although the sky was heavy with clouds. "You drove brilliantly despite the challenges of the muddy roads."

"We kept our heads and stuck to the pace notes," Daniel replied. "It helped that we ran early in each stage. The roads were slick, but they hadn't turned into quagmires yet."

"Even so," the emcee pressed, "there must be some secret to your success."

Daniel glanced at Frank across the car and refrained from mentioning his new relationship with his co-driver. It wasn't anyone else's business, even if he did think it had been a factor. "Having the paddle shifter in this car makes a huge difference," Daniel said, repeating his contention from the rally in Bulgaria. "My hands never have to leave the wheel."

"That sounds like a real plus," the emcee said. "So your win today puts you in first place overall as you head to Mexico in a few days. How does that feel?"

"I haven't really had a chance to think about it yet," Daniel admitted, "but I'm sure it will feel amazing once it sinks in. We had a really rough year last season, so it feels good to be competitive again."

"Well, congratulations on your win."

"Thank you," Daniel said, shaking the emcee's hand as he stepped back to make space for the rest of the Citroën team and the rally organizers with their bottles of champagne. The heavens chose that moment to open, drenching everyone with rain as thunder clapped overhead.

The spectators scattered, a few pulling out umbrellas, but most running for the nearest awning or overhang. Daniel threw his head back and let the water run down his face, laughing with the sheer delight of being number one in the world. It might not last past the next race, and even if it did, he had no delusions that Michaels would make the rest of the season easy for them, but for the next three weeks, until the rally in Mexico started, he and Frank would top the leader boards for the World Rally Championship.

"Get in the car," Frank said from the other side.

Daniel looked across the hood at his lover and laughed. "Why?"

"Because you're getting soaked, and Isabelle will skin us both if we mess up her precious car."

The threat of his sister's ire sobered Daniel's jubilation somewhat. He ducked into the car, knowing he was already soaked. "She'll forgive me," he told Frank as they pulled off the podium. "We're number one in the world right now. For that, she'll forgive me many things."

"Until Michaels beats us again," Frank laughed. "I'm not being pessimistic, but nobody wins every race."

"We're giving him a run for his money during what should have been a rebuilding season," Daniel said. "We're already ahead of the game for the year."

They drove back to the garage, meeting the rest of the team there. Everyone was as soaked as they were so Daniel figured Isabelle wouldn't be able to yell too much. The moment he stepped out of the car, she tackled him, only the frame behind him keeping him from landing on the ground. "You did it!" she squealed, kissing him on both cheeks. "I knew you could!"

"We did it," Daniel said, mindful of how much Frank had helped, keeping him steady, tweaking the pace notes on the fly to keep him under control in the changing weather conditions.

"Yes, you did," Jean-Paul said from behind Isabelle. He waited until she released her hold on Daniel before shaking the driver's hand. "I was worried after the way the shakedown went, but that seems to have knocked some sense into both of you. The weather didn't seem to bother you at all."

Jean-Paul hadn't seen Daniel's white knuckles during the race, but Daniel didn't argue. "We're soaked through," he said instead. "I know you'll want to organize a party, but do you mind waiting until we have a chance to get clean and dry first?"

"Of course," Jean-Paul said. "I'm sorry. I wasn't thinking. Take your time. We'll gather in the hotel lobby around seven. That gives everyone two hours to rest and shower. That should be sufficient."

Dismissed, the entire crew filed out of the garage. Tomorrow they'd be back at work, readying the car for transport to Mexico and the next rally, but tonight they would celebrate.

In the car that took them back to the hotel, Frank leaned over and whispered, "Two hours is more than enough time to shower."

Daniel grinned. "Not if we're sharing the shower, it isn't."

Frank chuckled. "I like the way your mind works. Your room or mine?"

"Mine has the condoms," Daniel reminded him, "unless you've stocked up since yesterday."

They had ended up in Frank's room after dinner the night before, only to realize Frank didn't have condoms. Not that it had stopped them from enjoying each other's bodies, but they didn't have to race tomorrow. It wouldn't matter if Daniel was sore in the morning, and he really wanted to feel Frank inside him again.

"Your room it is," Frank agreed. "As talented as your mouth is, I'm looking forward to getting reacquainted with other parts of you tonight."

"Get your kit and come to my room," Daniel said. "I'll leave the door open."

FRANK gathered his toiletries and a change of clothes, slipping them all into a bag for discretion, although he doubted it would fool anyone. He wasn't sure he cared about fooling anyone, to be honest. He was tired of hiding, especially now that he was on a team where his sexuality truly wasn't an issue. Sleeping with his driver might be an issue, but being gay wouldn't be.

He grinned as he worked, thinking about the past few days and all the changes they had wrought. He'd worried the entire time he was at home that he'd come back to a changed situation because of his aborted encounter with Dany before his abrupt departure. It hadn't been a planned departure, but that didn't change the fact that he had left. Dany's reception upon his return had been as cool as Frank had feared, up until Isa locked them in Dany's room. Since then, he and Dany had been pretty much inseparable. They'd slept in the same bed, eaten their meals together, even gone running together despite Dany's protests about getting up so early. He wouldn't be surprised if people had already started putting their new relationship together on their own. Frank wasn't planning on broadcasting it, but he didn't really want to hide either.

Despite his brave thoughts, he checked the hall to make sure it was empty before slipping into Dany's room. He knew his own feelings on the matter, but he didn't want to expose Dany to any more speculation than necessary without discussing it first. They had time, and their romantic relationship was still so new. Even if he'd been totally out and unconcerned about what anyone thought, he doubted he'd say much yet given how short a time they'd been together. Except it didn't feel like a short time. Between Frank's own fanboy crush and the months they had spent working together and becoming friends, it felt like they'd been together a lot more than four days.

"You don't look like you're in a celebrating mood," Dany said, coming out of the bathroom with only a towel around his waist.

"Just thinking," Frank said, summoning a smile. "It's hard to believe it's only been four days."

"It feels like more than that, doesn't it?" Dany chuckled. "I guess it's because we were already spending so much of our time together. The few additional hours hardly register."

"Other things register," Frank teased, determined to recapture the ebullient mood from their win. "Like the fact that I don't have to disguise my need to touch you behind massages any more. Do you need a massage before we go out?"

"I need a shower," Dany said. "I'm soaked and dirty, and you haven't even changed out of your jumpsuit. After we're warm and dry, we can discuss that backrub, although I can think of other places that will want some attention as well."

"I wasn't planning on waiting until we were dry for that," Frank said, urging Dany back into the bathroom. He dropped his bag on the floor but didn't bother searching for anything in it. Dany had shampoo he could use. He tugged on the towel, letting it drop to the floor and running his hands over Dany's body. Dany shivered against him.

"Your clothes are wet and cold," Dany complained. "Get undressed so we can get in the shower where it's warm."

"Start the water," Frank ordered with a swat to Dany's backside. "I'll be right there."

Dany squawked at the teasing slap, making Frank grin. He'd never seen the allure of really spanking a lover, but for that little noise, he might be tempted to try another swat or few. Dany started the water and disappeared behind the shower curtain, leaving Frank to undress as steam started to fill the room.

Tossing his clothes on the floor—they'd have to be washed before he could wear them again after the rain and mud from the rally—he climbed in the tub with Dany, running his hands down his lover's wet back.

Dany turned into his embrace, pulling Frank under the spray. After the cold, clammy clothes, the hot water almost hurt, but Frank let it wash over him, warming his skin. Dany's hands helped, too, rubbing over him insistently until the cold shivers stopped. He was shivering for an entirely different reason by the time Dany was done.

Frank pulled Dany back to his feet and into an embrace, lifting his head a little so he could reach Dany's mouth. Neither of them was particularly tall, but Dany had a couple of centimeters on Frank. Not that it mattered except for the logistics of lovemaking. Dany tipped his head obligingly, bringing their lips into full contact.

Frank slid his hands into Dany's water-sleek hair, combing through the longish strands as the kiss continued. Dany moaned softly, the sound spurring Frank to deepen the contact. He traced his tongue along Dany's full lower lip, relishing the way his lover's mouth opened to him. He took his time, licking and nipping at Dany's lips before moving in to explore his teeth and palate. Dany's tongue met his, tempting him deeper, but not vying for dominance.

They'd wrestled a bit their first couple of times in bed, working out the logistics of top and bottom, but Dany seemed to have settled into their roles now, giving Frank control without argument. Frank had no doubt that wouldn't last forever, but when that time came, they'd deal with it. Frank might prefer to top as a rule, but he'd bottom for the right man in the right set of circumstances. He suspected he'd found the right man. Now it was only a matter of circumstances.

Right now, though, he was the one in charge and he intended to take advantage of it. His hands roamed Dany's back and buttocks, keeping him close as they kissed, their chests and groins rubbing together voluptuously beneath the pounding spray. Frank kneaded the tense muscles, hoping to help Dany relax a little before they made love. Dany's groan and the way he bucked against Frank suggested Frank's efforts were having a different effect than he'd intended.

Frank reached between their bodies, his hand closing around both hard shafts. Dany bucked against him again. "Easy," Frank soothed, his free hand rubbing calmingly over Dany's back.

Dany shook his head. "Fuck me," he pleaded. "I'm flying too high for slow and sweet. We can do that later tonight. Right now I need you inside of me, pounding me into the wall."

"Turn around," Frank said, opening the shower curtain so he could retrieve one of the pre-lubed condoms. "Let's hope this is waterproof lube or this might hurt a bit."

Dany barked out a laugh. "I don't even care. Just fuck me already."

Frank chuckled as well, the desperation in Dany's voice spurring his own need. He rolled the condom on and worked a finger inside Dany. The muscle gave easily, tribute to how much Dany wanted this, just like this, right now.

Frank teased a bit longer, playing across Dany's prostate with deliberation until Dany was cursing and bucking beneath his hand. Giving one last flick to the sensitive nub, he pulled his fingers out and pressed the tip of his cock to Dany's entrance.

"Don't stop!" Dany protested when Frank rocked back and forth at his entrance.

"I'm not," Frank promised, "but I didn't exactly prep you, so I'm going to take my time now. I don't want to hurt you."

"Fuck—"

"Yes, I know," Frank interrupted. "Fuck that and fuck you. I will. When I'm good and ready."

Dany groaned in protest, but Frank soothed him by pressing a little deeper and licking up the line of his neck. "I know you're eager, baby," he murmured, rocking his hips against Dany's, each thrust taking him a little farther inside, "but I don't want to hurt you."

Dany moaned, the sound clearly one of pleasure this time. Frank steadied Dany's hips with one hand as he finally worked his way completely inside. The other hand mapped the contours of Dany's torso, stroking across his strong chest and down over washboard abs. Even when they'd lived together for those first few weeks after Frank arrived in France, he'd never seen Dany actually work out other than coming running with Frank occasionally, but nobody had a body like this without putting some work into it.

Frank's hand slid lower finally, his fingers teasing down the length of Dany's erection. Dany arched into the caress. Frank smiled and bit the spot where Dany's neck joined his shoulder. The howl that escaped Dany's throat at the nip of pain did wicked things to Frank's insides, so he bit down again, reaching between Dany's legs and cupping his sac at the same time. Dany's entire body froze at that, shivers racking him. Frank switched sides, biting the other shoulder and rolling Dany's balls with his fingers. That earned him a second howl and the onset of Dany's orgasm. It seemed to go on and on, the spasming muscles milking Frank's cock most deliciously.

Frank kept thrusting, harder now, trying to prolong Dany's release for as long as possible. Eventually, the pants and moans turned to whimpers. "Too much," Dany whispered.

Remembering their earlier conversation, Frank pulled back, his cock still aching for attention, but he didn't want to cause his lover any discomfort. He could jerk off with Dany's eyes on him, and that would be almost as satisfying as fucking him.

Dany had other ideas, apparently, turning around after only a moment. "Ditch the condom," he said, tweaking Frank's nipples.

Frank did as Dany said, waiting to see what else his lover had in mind.

It only took a minute to find out. Dany sank to his knees in front of Frank, urging him to lean back against the shower wall. Frank's eyes closed, not entirely sure he could handle to sight of his cock disappearing into Dany's mouth. They'd sucked each other off before this, but under the covers, sixty-nining so that Frank had been too occupied with Dany's cock to watch what Dany was doing to him. That wouldn't be the case this time. He'd either have to keep his eyes shut the entire time or deal with the highly erotic effects of watching.

To his surprise, Dany didn't go down on him right away, taking his time to titillate with caressing fingers. Frank groaned at the sensation, realizing that Dany was settling in to play. He had come already, giving him the control and patience to take his time now. Frank wasn't so lucky. "Don't wait too long, or I'll come all over your face instead of down your throat."

"How do you know that isn't what I want?" Dany teased.

Frank groaned at the decadent image of his spunk all over Dany's upturned face. His cock twitched at the thought.

"Looks like you like that idea," Dany said, his hand stroking Frank's erection with more determination now.

Frank shivered. "I like pretty much any idea that involves your hands or mouth on my cock."

Dany grinned and bent closer so he could lick the tip of Frank's cock. As he did, his hand slipped between Frank's legs, ghosting over his sac until his fingers pressed against Frank's entrance. "Even this one?"

Frank shivered again, parting his legs slightly. "I don't let just anyone do that."

"I know," Dany said, nuzzling Frank's iliac crease. "That makes it even better."

Frank's head fell back against the tiles as Dany worked a long finger deeper inside him and closed his mouth around the head of

Frank's shaft. Each time he tensed at the unfamiliar invasion of Dany's fingers, Dany would suck harder or work his tongue into the slit of Frank's cock, distracting him until he relaxed and Dany's finger could move deeper.

The entire situation could have been uncomfortable, but each time Frank thought he couldn't take any more, he would look down at the vision of Dany's lips stretched around his cock, a look of bliss on his face, and he would calm again, his nerves subsiding at the thought that this was Dany touching him this way, not some random stranger he'd picked up at a bar or a club. As long as he remembered that, he could give over some of his control and let Dany make love to him.

Dany found his prostate, rubbing the tip of his finger over it, surprising a yelp from Frank. Much to Frank's delight, Dany did it again, sending jolts of lust through Frank's system until he felt like his skin was about to explode because it couldn't possibly contain all the sensations coursing through him.

Dany tapped his gland one last time, drawing his cock deep into his mouth at the same time, and Frank lost all control, his release bubbling up and out of him to spill down Dany's waiting throat. He collapsed back against the wall, his knees giving out on him. Dany gathered him close, kissing him gently. "I think I like making you lose control."

Frank thought maybe he liked it too.

CHAPTER SEVENTEEN

A KNOCK on the hotel room door woke Daniel from a heavy sleep. He had to stop for a moment to get his bearings.

Right, Mexico. The shakedown was supposed to be today.

He thought for a second longer, ignoring the pounding at the door.

Yes, he was in his own room which meant he could answer the door. After he pulled on some clothes.

He dug around for a pair of boxers and T-shirt, figuring that covered him enough to answer the increasingly determined knocking.

"What?" he asked grumpily, opening the door as far as the security chain would allow. He didn't plan on letting anyone inside while Frank slept peacefully in his bed.

"Get a shower and meet me downstairs as quickly as you can," Jean-Paul ordered. "I got a phone call from WRC officials this morning saying Michaels has lodged a charge of illegal equipment against us. They want to check the car."

"That's bullshit!" Daniel said. "They check the car before every race. We haven't done anything illegal."

Jean-Paul shrugged. "That doesn't mean they won't check it again. And bring Frank with you."

"It's not what it looks like," Daniel stammered. "We were going over pace notes last night and fell asleep talking."

Jean-Paul rolled his eyes. "If you think you're fooling anyone with that excuse, you've got another thing coming." His hand stopped Daniel from closing the door. "This is serious, Daniel. I need you both downstairs fifteen minutes ago."

Daniel nodded. "We'll be there as fast as we can get in and out of the showers."

"Was that Jean-Paul?" Frank asked sleepily, sitting up in bed as Daniel closed the door.

"Yes," Daniel said, coming back to sit on the mattress next to Frank. "I told him we'd fallen asleep going over pace notes last night. I don't think he believed me."

"That might not be good," Frank said, rubbing his eyes. "What are we going to do?"

"That's the least of our worries at the moment," Daniel replied. "Michaels has accused us of cheating."

"What?" Frank cried indignantly. "How does he figure that?"

"Illegal modification to the car, apparently," Daniel said. "Look, we know there isn't anything illegal on our car unless he's found a way to plant something since last night. The only thing that's even unusual about our car is the paddle shifter, and Isa checked that out thoroughly as far as regs are concerned before she installed it. We'll be fine. We just have to go down and stand through the farce of the officials inspecting the car again to make sure we haven't changed anything since yesterday."

"I guess I should go back to my room and shower, then," Frank said. "It'll be faster that way, and I don't imagine Jean-Paul wants any delays."

"It'll also add credence to our story that you fell asleep here rather than planning to stay the night," Daniel agreed. "Jean-Paul doesn't believe it, I don't think, but we can keep up appearances while we're under the media scrutiny this cheating accusation is sure to bring."

Frank nodded, rising and walking across the room to where his clothes had landed the night before. Daniel stayed where he was, taking in the sight of his naked lover. Even under the circumstances and knowing they didn't have any time to waste, he couldn't keep from smiling at the little curl of desire that went through him. When Frank was dressed, Daniel caught his hand, pulling him into a swift embrace. "We'll get through this and we'll kick his ass again in the rally."

Frank took a deep, shuddering breath before he nodded. "Yeah, he won't know what hit him. He'll be eating our dust the rest of the week."

Daniel kissed Frank quickly and pushed him toward the door. "Meet me in the lobby as fast as you can get down there. That's where Jean-Paul told me to meet him too."

Alone in the room, Daniel stripped back off his dirty clothes and showered quickly, his thoughts racing as he considered the implications of the cheating accusation. He knew the officials wouldn't find anything, but the stain would be there, haunting them for the rest of the season. If they won, Michaels would continue to say they cheated, and if they lost, he'd say it was because they'd stopped cheating and couldn't keep up with him once they did.

The thought made him furious, but he pushed the anger aside. That wasn't his concern. His concern was driving to the best of his ability and doing everything he could to win the rest of the races. They had nine left. He needed to win one more than Michaels did if he wanted to take the championship for the season, assuming they both managed to finish every race.

Jean-Paul and the media team would worry about spinning whatever happened to protect the team's reputation. All Daniel had to do was keep winning so they'd have something to protect. Finishing his shower, he dressed quickly, taking the time to put on a shirt and slacks instead of a T-shirt and jeans like he usually wore to the garage. He doubted anyone would care how he looked, but there was no harm in looking presentable under the circumstances.

When he entered the lobby, he found Isabelle and Jean-Paul already waiting. Isabelle, too, had clearly taken more time with her appearance than usual. Jean-Paul always looked impeccable. "Frank should be down in a minute," Daniel said.

"He actually went to get coffee for us," Isabelle said. "He figured we'd all need it."

"So what now?" Daniel asked. "Besides waiting for Frank to get back, obviously."

"Now we go to the garage, let the officials check the car out, and declare we aren't cheating," Jean-Paul said. "We verified all the modifications we did on the car before we did them, and it's been inspected before every rally. This is an attempt to demoralize us, nothing more."

Privately Daniel worried it would work, but he didn't let any of his doubts show on his face. Frank came in before he could say anything else, four cups of coffee in hand. "Oh, good, you're here."

"Let's get this over with," Isabelle said, taking one of the Styrofoam cups from the cardboard carrier. "We still have work to do today."

When they reached the parc ferme, the race officials were already there along with Ryan Michaels, who looked so smug that Daniel wanted to put a fist in his face. That wouldn't help anything, so he settled for a glare at his rival. Michaels ignored him, as Daniel had known he would, his eyes fixed on Isabelle instead.

That was somewhat surprising, but Daniel left it alone for the moment. Isabelle could take care of herself, and given Michaels's accusation, she wouldn't be receptive to any interest on his part anyway. If what Daniel was seeing was actually interest and not something else.

The officials were all respectful and apologetic as Isabelle opened the gate to their section of the parc ferme and led everyone inside, but Daniel wasn't sure how much of that was real. Isabelle had done some innovative things on the new car, and while they had checked to make sure everything was legal, everything was certainly not standard.

They asked Isabelle to open the hood so they could inspect underneath, another nod to her sensibilities which Daniel appreciated even if Isabelle didn't. In her current mood, Isabelle wasn't appreciative of anything. She popped open the hood, revealing the souped-up engine and transmission. The officials stepped closer, beginning their inspection of the car. When they reached the paddle shifter, they paused to look at it, studying the mechanism in the transmission. "This connects to a paddle shifter on the steering wheel, correct?" one of them men asked Isabelle.

"Correct," Isabelle replied. "It's relatively new, but it's allowable under WRC regulations. We verified it before we even installed it."

"It is legal," the official agreed. "It's the first time I've seen one on an actual rally car, so I wanted to make sure I knew what I was looking at."

"What if she's lying?" Michaels interjected.

"Look, buster," Isabelle snarled, turning on him. Jean-Paul laid a restraining hand on her arm.

"We're hardly new to the sport," the official reminded Michaels. "This is clearly a modification to the transmission system which, if I follow these cables, leads directly to the paddle shifter installed on the steering wheel inside the cabin of the car. As a paddle shifter is legal under WRC regulations, the fact that I haven't seen one installed on a racing car before doesn't change anything. Now, we're here at your bchcst, but we made it very clear we would be the ones making the final ruling."

Isabelle shot Michaels a triumphant look as the officials continued their inspection of the car. After nearly half an hour, during which time Daniel did his best not to twitch nervously or reach for Frank's hand for comfort, the officials finally closed the hood. "Everything appears in order here. The car, while having some unusual modifications, meets all the regulations of the WRC. Mr. Monier, Mr. Leroux, Miss Leroux, thank you for your cooperation. We will see you at the shakedown run in a couple of hours."

Isabelle held her tongue until the officials had all left, Michaels trailing behind them, obviously reluctant to leave. The moment the race officials were out of hearing, Isabelle flew at Michaels. "You bastard," she hissed, backing him up against the wall. "How dare you make those kinds of accusations against us? Are you so insecure that you can't accept that we might actually beat you in a fair race?"

"I've finished ahead of you twice this season too," Michaels retorted, "and I don't care what the officials say. That paddle shifter is fishy."

"You're only saying that because I thought to install it on our car and your mechanic didn't. Don't blame me because you didn't hire competent people," Isabelle snapped. "Get the hell out of my garage. And don't think to come sniffing around here looking for more of our secrets. You're outmatched. Live with it."

She turned on her heel and marched off, leaving Michaels to stare after her in openmouthed silence. "Your sister is one hell of a woman," he said finally, turning to Daniel.

Daniel laughed. "Don't even think about it, Michaels. She'd eat you alive."

Michaels grinned. "Sounds like fun. Maybe I should go for it."

"After accusing her of cheating to win a race?" Daniel scoffed. "She won't give you the time of day."

"We'll see about that."

Frank's hand on Daniel's arm distracted him from any reply. He turned to see what his lover wanted, giving Michaels the opening he needed to disappear.

"What?" Daniel asked when Frank didn't say anything.

"It doesn't do any good to engage him," Frank said. "He's full of hot air, where the racing and where Isabelle are concerned. He's the kind that gets off on the argument."

"I wasn't arguing," Daniel said. "I was laughing at him."

"It's still a challenge to him," Frank insisted. "You don't think he can get Isabelle's attention so he'll do his damnedest to do it just to prove you wrong."

"Maybe I should warn Isabelle."

Frank stopped Daniel before he could take more than a step toward the garage. "In the mood she's in, she'll take your head off for even mentioning it, and I rather like your head where it is. Come on. You can warn her later after she calms down if it looks like he's seriously trying to make headway with her."

Daniel wasn't convinced, but he let Frank lead him back to the car so they could return to the hotel and change before the shakedown run later that morning. They had dressed for an inspection, not for a race, when they left the hotel that morning.

TWO hours later, back at the garage, fed and dressed to drive, they listened as Isabelle gave them a rundown on the last-minute tinkering she'd done. "I heard a suspicious rattle when I was checking the drive train this morning. I've tightened everything I can think of, but I want you to keep your ears open during the shakedown to see if anything seems off in the way the car handles or if you hear the same sound. I don't want to send you out there during the actual race in anything less than a perfectly smooth ride. The roads are treacherous enough without having to worry about the car."

"We'll pay attention," Daniel promised. "We certainly don't want a breakdown in the middle of a stage. Frank's good, but we can only carry so many tools in the trunk before the weight would slow us down."

"I'd say Frank's a whole lot better than good, given the smiles on your face since we left Australia," Isabelle quipped.

"Are we really that obvious?" Daniel asked. "Jean-Paul made a comment this morning about it too."

"No," Isabelle said. "You aren't obvious to anyone who isn't intimately familiar with your moods and behavior. I see it because I'm your sister. Jean-Paul sees it because of how well he knows you, but I'd bet most of the rest of the team hasn't noticed, and I'm sure no one outside the team has. When you're in the public eye, you act the same as you always have."

"We've certainly tried to be discreet about it," Frank agreed. "It's not anyone else's business."

"No, it isn't," Isabelle said, "although I think you could let the team in on it. They wouldn't care, and most of them would be happy for you."

"We'll tell them eventually," Daniel said. "We're not ready to share it with anyone really. Not yet. Even if they'd be happy for us, they'd still be watching us, and our personal relationship isn't their business."

"Not unless it starts affecting your job," Isabelle said.

"Has it yet?" Daniel demanded.

"If it has, it's only to make you an even better team than you were before," Isabelle replied. "Keep driving like you did in Australia and you'll take home the championship for sure."

"That's the plan," Daniel said with a grin.

"THEY'RE going to be watching our every move after Michaels's stunt," Frank warned as they pulled the car back into the garage after the shakedown run. "On the course and off, if only to make sure we don't try to sneak back in here and do something to the car during the night."

"They won't find anything," Daniel said, "because we aren't cheating."

"That's not what I meant," Frank said. "They're going to watch everything, not just the race time now. This could out us."

Daniel shrugged, not overly concerned at the prospect. "We've been discreet, and we have a long-established habit of going over pace notes the night before the race. No one will question that."

"They will if I don't return to my own room in time for us to both get a good night's sleep," Frank disagreed.

"Next time, we're getting a suite," Daniel decided. "That way nobody sees where we sleep or don't sleep."

"What about tonight?" Frank pressed.

Daniel hesitated for a moment, weighing the consequences of being found out against the displeasure of having Frank sleep in his own room. "We'll just have to hope they're more gullible than Jean-Paul if they're watching that closely."

"Do you really mean that?" Frank asked. "I won't be angry if you aren't ready to risk being open about us."

"We can't talk about this here," Daniel said, "unless you want to ask the rest of the team's opinions as well. We'll talk about it when we get back to the hotel. But yes, I really mean it."

They went through a thorough debriefing with Isabelle, answering all her questions and discussing her concerns. When everything was as ready as they could make it for the next day, they returned to the hotel. "Take a shower and then come to my room," Daniel said to Frank. "I'll order room service, we'll go over the pace notes for tomorrow, and we'll finish our conversation from earlier."

Frank nodded and let himself into his room. Daniel hurried down the hall to his own room, showering quickly and dressing again in comfortable clothes. He understood Frank's concern, but he really doubted it would come to that kind of scrutiny. If it did, the separate showers, the room service, and the casual clothes would hopefully give their evening an air of normalcy, a driver and co-driver prepping for a big race. And if it didn't, he'd meant what he said. He didn't care to flaunt his relationship with Frank, but he wouldn't deny it either.

He'd just called in an order for a meal when Frank knocked on the door and came in. "I ordered dinner," he said. "I figured a sampler platter would give us a choice of dishes. I love Mexican food, so anything you don't want, I'll gladly eat. They had this selection of regional specialties, *real* Mexican food."

"Fine with me," Frank said, opening the pace notes book. "Do you want to go over these now or after we eat?"

"After," Daniel said, tossing the book aside and pulling Frank to him. "We should finish our conversation from earlier first. That's far more important."

"More important than the race?" Frank asked, surprised.

Daniel nodded, not even needing to think about it. "You're a part of the race for me, so it's not a question of choosing between you and racing, not like it would be if I'd met someone in Clermont-Ferrand, but we're no good as a racing team if we aren't good here in private. Even when we were just friends, that was true. Now that we're lovers, it's more important than ever."

"Are you ready for people to know about us?" Frank asked, settling on Daniel's lap.

"Not in the sense of kissing you in public or talking about it to the press," Daniel replied honestly, "but that's more a question of preferring to keep my private life private. And yes, I know people say I gave that up when I chose a profession that puts me in the limelight, but that doesn't mean I have to make a spectacle of my love life. That said, if someone asks, I don't plan to deny it. Do you?"

"No!" Frank said. "But we hadn't talked about it, and there's never been any rumors about you being gay. I'd know if there had been."

Daniel looked at Frank sharply. "How closely have you been following my career?"

Frank flushed. "Since you started driving."

"It wasn't just the driving, was it?" Daniel asked, the coin dropping suddenly.

Frank looked away, the color on his cheeks darkening. "No. I've had a crush on you since I first saw your picture in a racing magazine six years ago. I've read every scrap of news or gossip I could get my hands on since."

"I'm flattered," Daniel said.

"Don't be," Frank retorted. "I was fascinated by a pretty face. Not that your talent hurt, but it was purely physical."

"And now?"

"Now it's real," Frank said. "Now I know you, so it isn't a crush anymore. It's genuine attraction and affection. If we're ready to answer honestly if we're asked, do we need to warn Jean-Paul? Out of courtesy, if nothing else."

"Probably," Daniel said, "but I'm not dealing with it tonight or tomorrow until after we're done racing for the day. We shouldn't have to deal with the press until tomorrow evening anyway, and if Jean-Paul is going to yell at us, I'd rather not have that on my mind while we're driving. I'm not looking forward to the second or third stages."

The room service waiter knocked at the door, interrupting them. He rolled a cart in when Daniel answered, uncovering the various dishes and telling them in halting English what each item was. Daniel thanked him with a generous tip and gestured for Frank to help himself.

Once they'd taken the edge off their hunger, Daniel tossed the pace book back to Frank. "All right, let's figure out how we're getting through those two stages without getting killed or losing the race."

Frank opened the book, picked up a pencil, and prepared to get to work.

CHAPTER EIGHTEEN

"RELAX," Frank ordered as they got out of the shower at the end of the next day's rallying. "You're so tense you won't be able to sleep tonight."

"I screwed up today," Dany said. "We're sitting in fourth place right now."

"You didn't screw up," Frank disagreed. "You didn't spin out, you didn't crash, you drove a clean race."

"And I still ended up in fourth place."

"Yeah, well, if it makes you feel any better, Michaels isn't winning either. If he takes third and we take fourth, it puts us tied for the season," Frank reminded Dany, rubbing soothingly at his lover's shoulders. "And today was the worst day as far as the stages go. You'll have a chance to recoup some of the lost time tomorrow and Saturday."

"I suppose I can always pray Michaels crashes," Dany said with a short laugh.

"Don't say things like that," Frank scolded gently. "It's bad karma to wish bad luck on someone else. Concentrate on what you can do instead."

"What can I do?" Dany said with a sigh.

"Stop that," Frank said, urging Dany into the bedroom. "Lie down. I'm going to work on your back and we're going to discuss tomorrow's stages."

Dany went with too much moroseness for Frank's peace of mind. His lover was taking the day's scores personally, far more so than he had in any of the other races, even the ones where Michaels beat him. Then again, in Sweden and Jordan both, he'd beaten his best times so he had a sense of triumph despite not finishing first. The course had changed here in Mexico so he had nothing to compare his times to, and while he had not made any mistakes on the second and third stages, his times had been poor compared to some of the other drivers. He'd recovered some of that in the later stages in the day, but not enough to rise above fourth place overall.

As his hands rubbed over the tense muscles of Dany's back, Frank bent and kissed the nape of his lover's neck tenderly. "You know this is just one race, right? And it's only the fifth one of the season. Even if we can't scrape our way out of fourth place, it's not the end of the world. Anything could happen between now and November."

"We were winning, though," Dany said. "It's been a long time since I've been in first place for more than the standings of a single race, even when I was driving with Christophe. I didn't expect it to hurt so much to lose that rank."

"Where is this defeatist attitude coming from?" Frank asked. "We still have two more days of racing left before you know what your final standing is in this rally and how that will affect your overall standing. Because nobody else is even close to us and Michaels, so as long as you finish ahead of him, you'll still be in first place for the season, and even if you finish behind him, the championship totals will still be obscenely close."

"I didn't drive like a champion today," Dany said, shifting a little beneath Frank's massaging hands, "and that bothers me far more than the numbers. No, I didn't make any mistakes, but I didn't show any genius either. I was run of the mill, no different than any of the other drivers out there."

Frank adjusted where he was kneading until Dany let out a shuddering breath. "Do you have to drive perfectly in every stage of every race?" he countered seriously. "I'm not saying you shouldn't try to do your best, but if you really did your best, isn't that enough?"

"Not when it puts me in fourth place," Dany said, rolling away from Frank's hands and onto his back. "I was distracted, worried about what the cheating allegation would do to us. I told myself I wouldn't let it bother me, that it was Jean-Paul's concern, not mine, but I couldn't stop thinking about it, and that's dangerous during a rally."

Frank couldn't argue with that. Distraction could get a driving team injured or killed. "So what can we do to make tomorrow better?"

"You could fuck me until I can't think straight," Dany replied.

"I could," Frank agreed, his body beginning to react at the suggestion, "but while that might help you sleep, I doubt it will help you concentrate tomorrow."

"No, probably not," Dany conceded.

"Did it not help to go through the pace notes last night?" Frank asked. "You've always said it did in the past, but if it's not working anymore, we can try something else."

"No, I don't want to stop doing that," Dany said. "I couldn't concentrate today, but I think it would've been even worse if we hadn't gone through the notes last night."

"Then we'll go through tomorrow's notes in a few minutes," Frank said. "What about during the race tomorrow? What are we going to do then?"

"Drive like hell," Dany said. "We have a leader to catch."

It was the answer Frank expected, but he wasn't entirely sure Dany was right. "Is it really worth that risk?"

"What?"

"Think about it," Frank insisted. "If we came in fourth, even if Michaels came in first, what would that do to us at this point in the season?"

"It would put us ten points behind him," Dany said.

"Ten points," Frank agreed. "Not ideal, but two more wins would make it up, even if he came in second in both races. Now what would happen if we crash?"

"It would put us twenty-two points behind him."

"Ten points or twenty-two points," Frank said slowly. "I'm not suggesting you drive less than your best. I would *never* suggest that you give less than your best, but there's a difference between driving your best and taking unnecessary risks. If it were the last race of the season, that would be one thing, but we still have eight races to go after this one. We have time to catch up from a small deficit."

Dany sighed. "I hate giving up without a fight."

"You aren't giving up," Frank said. "We'll go out there tomorrow and drive to the best of our abilities. If he makes a mistake, we'll take advantage of it. We'll do what we can to win, but we won't be the ones to make mistakes. He's hotheaded. You know he'll be cutting corners and taking shortcuts if he can. It might pay off for him, and he might end up in second or even first place instead of third, but it might backfire. And if he does, we'll be ready."

"SECOND again," Dany said, tossing his driving gloves on the hotel bed in frustration.

"Second, not fourth," Frank pointed out, trying not to lose his temper with Dany's negativity. They had driven flawlessly over the second and third day of the race, catching everyone except Michaels, who took risks at every turn and managed to pull farther ahead of them at each stage. Dany had consistently come in second on the stages by large enough margins to beat the leaders from the first day, but without ever catching Michaels. "Which means he's three points ahead of us right now. He's won two races, we've won two races. The only difference right now is the race in Sweden. You need to stop obsessing about this. You say it doesn't matter, but it does. It's affecting your attitude, and that affects your driving, no matter what you say."

"What am I supposed to think about?" Dany snapped. "It's my job to win races."

"And you have," Frank retorted. "Two first places, two second places, and one third place in five races is one hell of a record."

"Michaels's is better."

"Fuck Michaels's record," Frank all but shouted. "Take a shower. I can't talk to you when you're like this."

He turned and stormed out of the room, the door slamming behind him. He started toward his room, changing his mind as he passed Isabelle's door. He knocked on it instead.

"Frank?" Isabelle said when she opened the door. "What are you doing here?"

"I need some advice," he said with a heavy sigh. "I'm ready to strangle your brother, and since that would cost all of us our jobs, I really shouldn't do that."

"What's he done now?" Isabelle asked.

"He spends all his time thinking about beating Michaels."

Isabelle cocked an eyebrow at Frank. "And you can't distract him from that?"

"I don't mean when it's just us," Frank said, feeling his cheeks heat. "I mean while he's racing. He's lost sight of what he loves about the sport."

"So remind him," Isabelle said.

"How?"

"The rally is over. The car doesn't have to be strictly monitored now," Isabelle said. "Take the car, stuff him in your seat, and take him driving. Forget about times and pace notes and winning. Just drive. And if you grope him a bit at the same time, maybe it'll brighten his spirits all around."

"I don't have the keys."

Isabelle tossed them in Frank's direction. He caught them right before they hit him in the face. "Now get out of here. I need a shower, and I'm looking forward to getting to sleep late in the morning. Don't wreck the car. I don't want to have to explain this to Jean-Paul tomorrow." She winked as she pushed him toward the door.

Frank let her nudge him out into the hall, staring down at the keys in his hand as his thoughts raced. He wasn't as masterful a driver as Dany was, but he could handle the race car. He wasn't used to the paddle shifter, but the car had the regular gear shift still so he could use it instead. He could think of no real reason not to follow her advice, and if she was right and going for a drive for the fun of it helped, it would be worth it because Frank doubted his patience with Dany's current mood would last much longer.

Isabelle wasn't the only one who needed a shower, so instead of returning to Dany's room immediately, Frank went to his room, cleaning up quickly. This wasn't a date. He didn't have to look his absolute best, but he'd rather be freshly showered at least if he was able to talk Dany into a bit of car sex. Or car groping, anyway, since the racer didn't have a backseat to climb into.

Inspiration struck as he was dressing. He grabbed the spare blanket out of the hotel room closet. He could toss it in the trunk where they usually kept the tools and spare parts. If they found a quiet, private spot to stop and indulge, they'd be ready. He stuffed a couple of condoms and some lube in his pocket as well.

When he knocked on Dany's door a few minutes later, he didn't get an immediate answer. He knocked again, wondering if Dany had gone out without him. Dany answered the second knock, though, still dripping from his shower and dressed only in a towel. Frank was tempted to push him back inside and lick every droplet from his skin, but that wouldn't help with Dany's attitude. "Get dressed," Frank said. "We're going out."

"Out where?" Dany asked, his voice betraying his suspicion.

"That's a surprise," Frank said, "but you don't have to get dressed up. Comfortable clothes will be fine."

Dany's eyes narrowed even more as he stared at Frank for a minute, but eventually he relented, drying off and dressing quickly. "What's in the bag?"

"Nothing important," Frank said. "Relax and let me drive for a bit."

Dany looked like he wanted to keep arguing, but Frank ignored him, taking his arm and steering him toward the door. Dany shook his arm loose, but he kept moving in the direction Frank wanted, so he let it go, walking with Dany through the lobby of the hotel. When they hailed a cab and Frank gave the driver the address of the garage, Dany's face betrayed his surprise, but Frank shook his head.

"You realize we're going to get in trouble for this, don't you?" Dany said as they got out of the cab and walked toward the garage.

Frank grinned and dangled the keys Isabelle had given him in front of Dany's face. "Isabelle already knows. And if she's right with her suggestion, Jean-Paul won't care what we did because you'll be driving better, and that's his ultimate goal."

"You talked to Isa?" Dany asked.

"You were in a bad mood," Frank said with a shrug as he opened the door to the garage, "and I figured if anyone would know how to get you out of it, she would."

"So what did she suggest?"

"I already told you it's a surprise," Frank said, "although obviously we're going for a drive."

Dany walked toward the driver's side of the car, but Frank caught his arm. "Not tonight. Tonight you get to sit in the other seat. It's my turn to drive."

"You think you can handle it?" Dany said.

Frank started to retort hotly when he caught sight of the grin on Dany's face. Teasing was better than sulking. "Oh, I know I can handle it," Frank said. "Your car will purr for me just like you do."

It was Dany's turn to struggle for a retort, the momentary silence long enough for Frank to slip into the driver's seat. "Come on, you're wasting time."

Dany scowled at that but took the passenger seat as Frank started the car and eased it out of the garage. He watched his speed while they were within the more populated areas, but once they cleared the city limits and headed out into the desert, he rolled the windows down and increased his speed. He didn't push the way Dany did when they were racing because it was dark and he didn't have pace notes for Dany to read, but he drove faster than he would have in a different car. The wind rushed around them, bringing the cool breeze off the desert mountains and the sandy smell that nothing else could imitate.

"Close your eyes," Frank suggested. "Don't think about where we are or where we're going or anything other than the fact that we're here."

Dany looked hesitant, but as the minutes passed with nothing else to do, his eyes drifted shut. Frank slowed slightly, starting to look for a place to pull off the road now that Dany was letting go of some of his tension. It would take more than such a short drive to release all of it, but they had to start somewhere.

Seeing an outcropping of rock, Frank pulled the car carefully off the road. The suspension was built to handle more bumps and ditches than the average car, but it wasn't an off-road vehicle, and he didn't want to repay Isabelle by creating more work for her when they got back. With a little skill and a lot of luck, he managed to pull the car off the tarmac and mostly out of sight of the road. Dany's eyes opened slowly. "What are we doing here?"

"Relaxing," Frank said, climbing out of the car and spreading the blanket across the sand. "Come sit with me and look at the stars."

"You're crazy," Dany said, but he joined Frank on the blanket, reclining somewhat so he could stare at the stars wheeling overhead. "Is there a reason behind this jaunt into the country?"

"Does there need to be?" Frank asked seriously. "We can't simply decide to go for a drive because we feel like it?"

"We spend large portions of our lives in a car," Dany said. "Somehow I didn't envision spending my leisure time in one as well."

"That's the problem, I think," Frank said. "I remember watching you drive and always feeling like you got such joy from racing. You aren't joyful now. You're tense and stressed and obsessed with beating Michaels instead of relaxed and enjoying your job. I thought maybe a little drive for pleasure would remind you of what you love about this sport."

"It's the adrenaline high," Dany said immediately. "It's not knowing from one second to the next exactly what's going to happen. Sure, I have the pace notes, but it's still uncertain."

"You've forgotten how to enjoy that," Frank insisted. "Maybe driving out here tonight and then back won't remedy that completely since we don't have pace notes and can't push the limits of the car's capabilities in the dark this way, but maybe it will remind you a little. And if it does, we can see about coming back out here in the daylight and driving like mad for the pure pleasure of it."

Dany nodded slowly, falling silent at Frank's side. Frank let the silence stretch. Dany needed to relax, not to listen to him nag. He could feel the tension in his lover's frame easing slowly in the way his shoulders unscrunched and his foot stopped bouncing back and forth. When Dany had settled, Frank pounced, pulling open Dany's jeans and swallowing his soft cock in one gulp. Dany's shout echoed through the mountains, but Frank ignored it. There was no one around for miles to hear them.

WHEN Frank finally lifted his head, Dany lay limp and panting on the blanket beneath him. Rolling to his side, ignoring his own erection, Frank fished the keys from his pocket and tossed them on Dany's bare stomach. "You get to drive back to the hotel."

Dany turned his head in Frank's general direction. "In what world is that a good idea?"

"In the one where you love to drive," Frank reminded him. "Forget about everything but how good it feels to have a powerful, responsive car beneath your hands."

"I'd rather have a responsive lover beneath my hands."

Frank grinned. "Drive me back to the hotel and you can have whatever you want."

CHAPTER
NINETEEN

"WHY do they have rallies in the hot countries in the summer and in the cold countries in the winter?" Frank complained as he pulled on his protective gear prior to the start of the first stage in Portugal.

"It's only May," Daniel reminded him. "They could have scheduled the rally for August."

"Like Greece in August is any better."

Daniel laughed and glanced around to make sure they were alone before kissing Frank quickly. He wasn't ashamed of the growing feelings for his lover, but he didn't consider them anyone else's business, and if any of the crew saw them kissing, they'd have questions at the least. This way they avoided that altogether.

The past three weeks had been a revelation for Daniel. The euphoria of being ahead in the championship had colored the break between the Australian and Mexican rallies, and that had carried over to his interactions with Frank, everything very light and easygoing and jovial. The frustration of the cheating allegation and then falling back into second place had cooled the euphoria, returning Daniel's mood more to business as usual, with the exception of his time with Frank.

In the midst of all the publicity appearances and moving the cars back to Europe and everything else that was involved in their jobs, Frank had dragged Daniel away for at least an hour every day to take a car—any car, not even always a race car—and go for a drive. After their night in the Mexican mountains, Frank hadn't insisted on driving again, letting Daniel take control instead. It had worked wonders for Daniel's mood, reminding him of the freedom, the joy, the *fun* of pitting his skill against the laws of physics. Through it all, through the frustration and the strategy meetings and the publicity appearances and all the rigmarole that made up Daniel's life, Frank had been a solid, supportive presence at his side.

He was ready for the Portugal rally because Frank had made him so.

"Let's do this," Daniel said, pulling on his helmet. "We have fans to impress."

Frank nodded and pulled on his own helmet, climbing into the other side of the car as Daniel got settled and fixed his safety harness. One of the things that had come out of the long drives and the long conversations that punctuated them was the reason Daniel had started in the sport and stayed in it. He loved the fans who came to the rallies and cheered for all the drivers, win or lose. They helped flip cars back over or pushed them out of ditches when they had a wreck. They checked on the drivers and co-drivers of every car that needed help, regardless of language, nationality, or standing. The people who came to watch the rallies loved cars and racing the same way Daniel did, and win or lose, he was determined to give them a good show. He might not like signing autographs, but here, in the car, he could give people what they wanted without hesitation. The rest, while still important, had become secondary again, the way it needed to be for him to focus on the driving, not the winning.

They pulled up to the starting line at the first stage, Michaels's tail lights disappearing around the first curve. Daniel ignored the urge to chase after the other car and prove once and for all that he was the better driver. Rallies didn't work that way. The countdown on the start clock began, and Daniel put the car in gear, revving the engine as the count neared zero. The moment it did, he released the brake and flew down the first stretch, following Frank's directions with an automation that might have been frightening if he hadn't trusted Frank so implicitly.

As they neared the first bend, Daniel pulled on the paddle shifter to move to a lower gear in preparation for coming out of the bend and accelerating as quickly as possible down the straight stretch beyond it.

Nothing happened.

"*Merde*," he cursed, pulling on the paddle shifter again.

"What's wrong?" Frank demanded.

"The paddle shifter went out." Even as he spoke, he dropped one hand from the wheel to the stick shift between their seats, changing gears and resuming the rhythm of the drive. His mind still reacted automatically to Frank's directions, but his body had lost the feel of driving with the gear shift instead of the paddle shifter, and it slowed his reflexes, only one hand on the wheel for short intervals of time when he had to fight harder to keep the car under his control.

They finished the first stage with a respectable time, but Daniel worried they'd be hard pressed to maintain it over the day's race if they couldn't fix it. They couldn't return to the service park until another three stages were complete, but the rules didn't prevent him and Frank from doing their best to fix the paddle shifter between stages.

"Go to the start of the next stage," Frank said when Daniel started to pull over. "We'll look at it there. We don't want to be late for the next start and have a time penalty."

Seeing the logic of Frank's suggestion, Daniel drove to the next stage as quickly as allowed. Off the closed courses, they were expected to obey all posted speed limits and road regulations.

"Problems?" Michaels drawled when they reached the next stage and jumped out of the car to examine the transmission.

"Shut up, Michaels," Daniel growled as he searched for the cause of the paddle shifter's failure. "Fuck!" he muttered when he found it. "Look at this, Frank."

Frank looked at the wire in Daniel's hand. "That looks like someone cut it."

"Yeah, I don't think this was an accident."

"It'll be awful hard to win without your 'secret weapon'," Michaels mocked as he got back in his car to begin the next stage. "Eat my dust, loser."

Daniel took a step toward Michaels's car, but Frank caught his arm before he could do anything rash. "Let it go," Frank said. "You beat him two years ago even without the paddle shifter. You can do it again. And maybe Isabelle can fix it tonight, even if she can't fix it during the service park after the third stage."

"It'll be our turn next," Daniel said, pushing aside all thought of sabotage and Michaels's superiority complex. He couldn't afford to be distracted by any of that now. He had a race to run. He might not win with his slowed reaction time, but he had to stay close enough that he had a chance of pulling out a win once Isabelle fixed the paddle shifter.

After the shock of the mechanism not working passed, Daniel found it easier to go back to the regular gear shift as the subsequent stages went on. If he wasn't quite as fast as with the paddle shifter, that was the nature of the two systems. He thought his times were respectable.

The moment they hit the service park, Isabelle came running.

"Don't worry about the usual stuff," Daniel said, pulling off his helmet. "The paddle shifter isn't working. It looks like someone sabotaged it."

"What?" Isabelle said. "Pop the hood."

"It's already open," Daniel said, waiting for her to lift the hood so he could show her the damage he'd found. "Fortunately they didn't damage the regular gear shift, so I could still drive, just a little slower than has become my habit."

Isabelle looked at the mess in his hands. "I can fix it, but not in time for your next stage. Maybe tonight, depending on how strict they are with the evening service park."

"Okay," Daniel said, mentally reevaluating his strategy for the day. "Take care of the usual stuff, then, and tell Jean-Paul what's going on while Frank and I are out at the next stage. I don't know how anyone got in last night, but it was working fine during the shakedown run yesterday. We don't want there to be any more damage tonight."

"I'll tell him," Isabelle said, her focus clearly back on getting the car ready to run the next three stages.

Daniel stepped back and let her work. "We'll have to finish the day without the paddle shifter and hope she can fix it tonight," he told Frank.

"So that's what we'll do," Frank replied. "Mechanical problems are part of the job. Granted, this one was intentional rather than accidental, but that's not our concern. Our concern is what it always has been."

"Getting the best time possible," Daniel said. "I know. I'm angry it happened, but I'm not going to lose focus because of it."

"Hit the road!" Isabelle called, drawing their attention back to the car. "Drive safely. Even if it means taking a hit on the time. You're not used to the regular gear shift in this car. Don't take unnecessary chances."

"We'll be careful," Daniel promised, giving Isabelle a quick kiss on the cheek before he pulled his helmet back on. "Thank you, *p'tite sœur*."

"Get out of here," Isabelle said, pushing him toward the car.

"DON'T even tell me what place I'm in," Daniel said as he met Jean-Paul at the service park at the end of the day. "I don't want to know."

"I'm not worried about that," Jean-Paul agreed. "I'm worried about the fact that someone tampered with the car during the night in what was supposedly a secure area."

"I didn't dream it up," Daniel said.

"I didn't say you did. If you and Isabelle tell me someone tampered with the car, I believe you," Jean-Paul replied. "The rally officials may be a little harder to convince, but I'm behind you one hundred percent."

"So what happens now?"

"I filed a complaint and a sabotage report with the rally officials. They'll be here in a few minutes to look at the evidence," Jean-Paul said, "and then they'll have to decide if they want to involve the local police. It's not as if we have any suspects."

"We have one," Daniel muttered, thinking about Michaels and the obnoxious comments he'd made at every turn today. "Michaels has gloated all day long about the paddle shifter being broken."

"When did he make the first comment?" Jean-Paul asked.

"After the first stage," Daniel replied. "He was there when we found the damage and realized it wasn't accidental. He made a comment about us being second-best without our secret weapon, or something like that."

"So he knew what was wrong without you telling him?"

"I certainly didn't look at him and say 'the paddle shifter is broken' but that doesn't mean he didn't overhear my conversation with Frank or that he couldn't tell what part of the engine we were looking at and make an educated guess," Daniel said. "I'd love for him to be the one responsible because then he'd forfeit this race and maybe be suspended for the rest of the season, but that doesn't mean he is the culprit."

"So if not him, then who?" Jean-Paul asked.

Daniel shrugged. "Who knows? A disgruntled fan, a crooked official, a dissatisfied mechanic, a homophobe who found out about Frank. The list is endless."

"That isn't going to help the rally officials or the police," Jean-Paul reminded him.

"That's their problem," Daniel replied. "Mine is finishing this race in a sabotaged car and hoping I can do well enough not to fall too far behind for the season. Look, unless you need me here, I'm going to take a shower and get something to eat. It's miserably hot under all this protective gear, and I'm famished. I didn't eat much lunch today."

"Go," Jean-Paul said. "I'll come by your room later and tell you what they said."

"Tell me in the morning," Daniel said, not wanting Jean-Paul to interrupt his evening with Frank. He needed that island of tranquility after the day they'd had. "I need to think about something else tonight."

Jean-Paul didn't argue, although Daniel had the feeling he wanted to. Daniel found Frank waiting for him outside, already out of his coveralls and looking incredibly sexy with the wind ruffling his disheveled hair. "Can we talk about it in the morning?" he asked, knowing Frank had to be bursting with questions.

"I wasn't planning on anything else," Frank said. "We both need showers. You need a backrub, and then we need to look at tomorrow's pace notes. Nothing else matters tonight."

The return of that comfortable routine settled Daniel's frazzled nerves. "Thank you," he said. "It's nice that some things never change."

Frank threw a companionable arm around Daniel's shoulders as they walked back to the hotel a short distance from the garage. "Some things never will."

"Do you mean that?" Daniel asked, looking over at Frank, his heart pounding in his chest.

"Absolutely," Frank replied, his hand squeezing Daniel's shoulder lightly. "We make a good team, on and off the track."

"I guess we do at that," Daniel said. They reached the hotel. "Do you need to go back to your room?" Jean-Paul still paid for two rooms, although Daniel had considered telling him not to bother, but as long as they maintained the fiction of being only racing partners, they couldn't ditch the second room.

"Only for a minute," Frank said. "I'd like to get some clean clothes to put on."

"You should just bring your suitcase to my room," Daniel complained. "Then you wouldn't have to keep going back and forth."

"We need connecting rooms," Frank agreed. "Then we could be together and still maintain appearances."

Daniel didn't answer as Frank disappeared into his room. His annoyance at having to maintain appearances increased as he let himself into his room and waited for Frank to join him. He didn't particularly relish the firestorm of publicity that would surround their coming out. They'd had enough publicity for the season with the cheating allegation and now the sabotage. He didn't want to add to that, but they could tell Jean-Paul and maybe the rest of the team. The confidentiality clause in everyone's contracts would keep them quiet about it, not that he actually expected any of them to go running to the media.

"What are you thinking about so hard?" Frank asked, coming into the room and shutting the door behind him. "I can practically see the steam coming out of your ears."

"Nothing," Daniel said, turning in Frank's embrace and resting against his lover's body for a moment. It felt so good to be held that way. He took a deep breath, undisturbed by the smell of sweat rising from Frank's body. He knew he smelled the same way. Far more important was the sense of peace that settled over him as he stood there, feeling safe from the outside world suddenly. Tomorrow would be what it would be, but at this moment, with Frank's arms around him, he felt like he could face anything. The moment stretched, neither of them making any move to pull apart. Emotions surged through Daniel, welling up inside him until he had to give them voice. "I love you," he said, lifting his head so he could meet Frank's eyes. "I thought I should probably tell you that."

Daniel could see the surprise flit across Frank's face. "You don't have to say it back," Daniel said quickly. "I know it's fast, but I needed to say it and—"

Frank's lips closed over Daniel's, ending the spate of nervous words. The feeling of Frank's tongue surging into his mouth eased Daniel's fears. Frank couldn't hear that declaration and kiss him this way if he didn't feel something in return.

"Did anyone ever tell you that you talk too much?" Frank asked when he finally ended the kiss.

Daniel shook his head.

"Well, you do. If you'd let me get a word in edgewise, I could have told you I love you too. I have for a while, but I didn't say anything because it seemed too sudden or too much like a carryover from the crush I had on you before I ever met you."

Daniel's eyes widened at that, but he kept his mouth firmly shut, not wanting to stop the flow of Frank's words.

"You've been the star in my private fantasies since you started driving," Frank continued. He'd told Daniel that once before, but Daniel didn't interrupt to mention that either. "The call to come interview with you was a dream come true, and you're even better looking and more charismatic in person than you are on TV. I thought I'd died and gone to heaven, except we couldn't be together."

"We can be," Daniel disagreed. "That's what I was thinking about when you came in. I want to tell Jean-Paul and end the charade with two rooms. I've slept better since you started staying with me than I have in years. It's like having your arms around me makes up for being in an unfamiliar bed night after night. I'm tired of hiding what you mean to me."

"You want to come out?"

"Not to the general public," Daniel said quickly. "Not at the moment, anyway. I'd rather let the hoopla die down for a bit first, but yes, I want to come out to Jean-Paul and maybe to the rest of the team, depending on what he and Isabelle think. I can't see the future, but we work well together, we live well together. If we can do those things with the pressure of racing on us, I think we can do them all the time. We're already partners."

"Relationships are hard work."

"I know that," Daniel said. "I do. That's why I've always avoided them, because I wasn't ready to put the work in or sure that the person I was with was ready. I don't feel that way now. We've already proven we can work together, and not just work together, but work together spectacularly well. I have never been as centered, in or out of the car, as I have been since you came along. You walked in here just now and everything suddenly felt right again instead of feeling tense. You put your arms around me and I relaxed. If you feel the same way when you're with me, then we've got it made."

Frank's arms tightened. "We've got it made."

CHAPTER TWENTY

THE third place in Portugal was hard to take, putting them behind by thirteen points for the season, but Daniel consoled himself with the fact that Jean-Paul had been perfectly sanguine when they told him to stop wasting money on two hotel rooms since they were only sleeping in one anyway. The rally officials hadn't found anything to lead them to the saboteur, but they had allowed Jean-Paul to leave a team member on watch outside the garage during the night to make sure no additional tampering occurred. Daniel felt sorry for the guys who got stuck with night duty, but they all assured him it was better than having the car disabled during the next day's stages.

The move from Portugal to Italy had been an easy one, actually allowing Daniel and Frank a few days off. They'd taken advantage of them, spending the time at Daniel's cousin's house on the Mediterranean coast, outside of Narbonne. They'd lazed around on the beaches where no one knew them and spent one day in Carcassonne, exploring the medieval city. When they arrived on the island of Sardinia, they were tanned and refreshed and ready to take back the lead.

"I got the paddle shifter repaired during the break," Isabelle said when Frank and Daniel joined her at the garage before the shakedown run, "and the rally officials here said we can have someone at the garage at all times."

"Good," Daniel said. "Let's see how the shakedown run goes and if there are any tweaks we need to make."

"There shouldn't be since it was simply a question of replacing the damaged cables," Isabelle said, "but definitely let me know if anything feels off."

Daniel wouldn't have admitted to the apprehension he felt as he started through the shakedown stage, always worried the paddle shifter would fail again. It didn't, fortunately, but he had a feeling he'd driven more conservatively than usual.

"Did everything work normally?" Isabelle asked the moment they finished the course.

"Fine," Daniel said.

"You didn't look like you were driving as aggressively as usual, even for a shakedown," Isabelle said. "Are you sure the car wasn't having problems?"

"I'm sure," Daniel said. "I didn't see any reason to push it to the limits. If it works, it works."

Isabelle didn't look convinced, but she let it go. "Get a good night's sleep," she said, fixing Frank with a firm stare too. "You need to be fresh in the morning."

"We will," Frank said before Daniel could reply, steering him away from Isabelle.

"She's going to tease us every chance she gets," Daniel complained.

"It was your idea to do away with the charade of separate rooms," Frank replied with a laugh. "You can't have it both ways."

"Sure I can," Daniel said. "I can tell her to stuff it."

"You can try."

Daniel scowled when Frank's laughter only got louder. The annoyance faded when they reached the floor of the hotel Jean-Paul had reserved for the Citroën team. He pulled out the key to their one room and let them inside. Both suitcases sat against the far wall, placed there by the hotel valet. "Look, honey, we're home," Daniel joked to cover the surge of emotion he felt at being at a rally and still able to share a room with Frank.

"Maybe not quite 'home' but definitely the next best thing," Frank agreed, letting the door shut behind him and pulling Daniel into his arms. Daniel leaned back against him, relaxing completely in the tender embrace.

DANIEL hit the accelerator as the starter reached zero on the third stage of the first day, tires spinning on the gravel as they hit the first bend. The drives for pleasure in Mexico and the break from everything related to racing had given Daniel back his edge, and they were a couple of seconds ahead at the start of the third stage. He refused to focus on that, concentrating instead on driving his best.

They were five minutes into an eighteen-minute stage when they came around a bend to see Michaels's Evo Lancer on the side of the road.

"What the hell?" Daniel muttered.

"Who cares?" Frank replied. "Keep driving."

Daniel nodded and turned his attention back to the road in front of them, cresting the hill with a spray of gravel as the tires left the ground for a moment to the cheers of the assembled fans. Daniel couldn't stop the burst of excitement at the knowledge that their time would be at least two minutes faster than Michaels since he had started the stage two minutes before them and was now some distance behind them. He'd try not to be too gleeful when they all reached the service park at the end of this stage, but after the man's obnoxious comments at the last two rallies, it would be hard not to gloat a little.

"What happened?" Isabelle asked as soon as they pulled into the service park at the end of the third stage. "Michaels hasn't come back in yet."

"We passed him about five minutes in," Daniel said. "They had the hood up and were doing something. We didn't stop to check what the problem was."

"Of course not," Isabelle said. "That's not like his team, to let something slip by them. Do you think the same person who got us last rally got him this time?"

"I thought you thought his team was responsible," Daniel said.

Isabelle shrugged. "He makes a convenient scapegoat, but I don't really think he'd stoop that low. He wants to win, but if he cheated that way, he'd have to live with knowing he couldn't win on his own merits. And furthermore, since we made public the sabotage, everyone else would always wonder if he would have won if we hadn't been hit."

"True." Before Daniel could say more, Michaels came barreling into the service area, shoving Daniel backward.

"I told you in Portugal I had nothing to do with the sabotage to your car," Michaels shouted. "You took revenge on the wrong man."

"What are you talking about?" Daniel shouted back, fairly sure he'd understood the angry rush of words in the weakest of his three languages.

"We didn't do anything," Frank said, coming to Daniel's side, his hand on Daniel's elbow helping Daniel keep his temper under control. "If something happened to your car, you need to report it to the authorities just like we did. If it was deliberate, then it might be the same person who damaged the paddle shifter on our car."

"Someone loosened one of the plugs so the oil leaked out over the course of the race," Michaels said.

"Are you sure it was intentional and not a question of a plug simply coming loose?" Frank asked. "I'm not saying your mechanics didn't do their job, but stuff happens."

"My head mechanic swears he checked them all last night," Michaels said, his voice calming as Frank kept his calm.

"Then you need to report it to the race officials," Isabelle said. "This makes two races in a row where one of the top contenders has suffered damage to a car. That isn't right."

"I thought you blamed me for your damage," Michaels said bitterly.

"No," Isabelle said. "Your win would be hollow if it took sabotage to beat us. Besides, you've proven you can win without it, just as we have proven we can win. We didn't need to sabotage you to win in Bulgaria. You didn't need to sabotage us to win in Jordan. Whoever is doing this, it is no one here."

"So who could it be?" Frank asked seriously. "I thought perhaps it was a gay bashing since it started after Dany and I got together, but while that would explain the tampering with our car, it wouldn't explain someone tampering with your car."

Daniel might have laughed at the comic expression on Michaels's face if it hadn't been for the seriousness of the conversation. He hadn't planned on telling anyone outside their team right away, but he and Frank had also agreed not to deny it if asked. Michaels hadn't exactly asked, but it was germane given the repeated sabotage. He glanced questioningly at Frank, who shrugged and then nodded. Daniel let it go for now. Whatever Frank's reasons for outing them this way, it hadn't been accidental. Daniel could ask for details later.

"No, it doesn't explain tampering with my car," Michaels agreed after a moment. "Nor does it justify the damage done to your car. Just for the record, you know."

"This can be a pretty homophobic sport," Frank said.

Michaels shrugged. "That doesn't mean we're all assholes. My best friend is gay. It may not be a persuasion I share, but it isn't one that bothers me. Just don't, you know, start making out in front of me or anything, okay?"

Daniel offered Michaels his hand. "Deal. If you think it would help, we could go with you to report the sabotage to the race officials, to try to persuade them this isn't an isolated incident."

"We don't know that it isn't," Isabelle said. "It certainly seems odd to have it happen two races in a row this way, but we have no way of connecting the two incidents except our suspicions."

"And the fact that Garza took second in Portugal and is now in second here in Italy," Michaels pointed out. "If he keeps that up, he could be in contention for the title."

"But he only beat me in Portugal, and there's no guarantee he'll be able to beat you now that the oil leak is fixed in your car," Daniel replied. "I'm not saying it isn't him, but it seems like an awfully big gamble for very little payoff given how far behind us he is right now. Second in Portugal is the highest he's finished because you and I have come in first and second except for in Finland, and he was behind us there too."

"We won't solve anything by speculating," Frank agreed. "Let's go report the sabotage and let the officials worry about it. We don't have much time until the next round of stages."

ISABELLE bent over the hood of Michaels's car alongside his head mechanic and the race officials. Frank held back, not wanting to add another head or another opinion to the ones already involved in the investigation. The rally officials had taken the charge of sabotage very seriously, ordering a delay to the start of the next stage until they could investigate. They also encouraged all the other mechanics to check their cars to make sure there weren't other cases of sabotage that hadn't yet been discovered.

"Michaels is totally checking her out instead of paying attention to what the officials are saying," Frank whispered to Dany.

"He is," Dany agreed, his voice amused, much to Frank's relief. He didn't want to add any more tension to the already tense situation.

"That's why I told him," Frank added, now that he knew Dany wasn't disturbed by Michaels's interest in Isabelle. "I suspect we'll be seeing a lot more of him off the race course, and I thought it would be better to tell him ourselves than have him stumble on it and think he had blackmail material on us."

"Makes sense," Dany agreed. "Do you think the two cases are related?"

"I don't know what to think," Frank admitted. "I hate to think someone is sabotaging cars at all. It was bad enough when it happened once, but to think it happened again is even worse. And to have it hit two different drivers. It doesn't make sense."

"It didn't make sense to begin with," Dany said. "The only person who gained anything from our problems in the last race is now the target of the sabotage in this one."

"You don't think he was responsible anymore?" Frank asked.

"Isa's right," Dany said with a shake of his head. "He was a convenient scapegoat, but it's not his style, and I don't really think it was a case of gay bashing because no one knew about us, although I guess they could have found out about you from your previous driver. Which leaves me with nothing."

"Look at this," Isabelle said, standing up from where she'd bent over Michaels's car. "The threads on the plug are worn down. If this were a random car off the street, I'd scold the driver for letting the plugs get in this condition, but this isn't a random car. No racing mechanic would leave a plug like this in a car."

"So what are you saying?" Michaels asked.

"Either someone deliberately installed an old plug or someone filed down the threads so the plug would work loose during the race," she replied. "I'd go with filing down the threads because the visible portion of the plug doesn't look old."

"So it wouldn't tip me off," Michaels's mechanic said, finishing Isabelle's thought. "We had a service park this morning before the race started. A short one, to be sure, but a chance to check things out visually. If I'd seen an old plug, I'd have changed it out, but I didn't take out every plug to check them because I knew I installed new ones after Portugal."

"So what do we do now?" Michaels asked.

"We've already arranged extra security for the rally," Dany said. "If no one has a problem with it, you could put your car in with ours during the night to make sure it isn't tampered with again during this race. That gives you a little breathing room to figure out your own extra security. If you're willing to trust us."

"Your sister has her head under the hood of my car," Michaels said with a laugh and an admiring glance in her direction. "If I was worried about trusting you, that would be a lot more dangerous to me than having my car in your garage for the night. If she's as good as her reputation suggests, she knows everything there is to know about my car at this point."

"Oh, she's better," Dany said with a grin. "And she won't let you forget it, either."

"He's smarter than he looks," Isabelle said from beneath the hood of the car, lifting her head and sending Michaels a warm smile despite the bite in her words. "He appreciates a good thing when he sees it."

Frank stifled a chuckle. Apparently Isabelle had it as bad as Michaels did.

CHAPTER TWENTY-ONE

POUNDING on the hotel room door roused Frank from sleep. He pulled on a pair of boxers and made sure Dany was decently covered before he answered. Jean-Paul stood outside. "They've caught the saboteur," he announced. "Get dressed and come downstairs."

"Do we have time for a shower?" Frank asked, not entirely sure he wanted to deal with the press without cleaning up first.

"As long as you hurry," Jean-Paul said.

Frank nodded and shut the door, going back to the bed to wake Dany. They had made it through three races with no more sabotage on their car, on Ryan's car, or on anyone else's to the best of their knowledge, bringing them to Alsace and the French rally. Frank still chuckled every time he thought of Ryan Michaels and the change the past two months had brought. He was still their rival on the race course, but he had become a regular fixture in their garage, at their table, and, he was pretty sure, in Isabelle's bed. He hadn't actually caught one of them coming out of the other one's room, but he had surprised them making out in the back of the garage. They'd pulled apart at his discreet cough, but Isabelle's expression had all but dared him to make a comment. He hadn't.

Dany had been a little less sanguine about it, but Frank figured he'd get over it as long as Isabelle stayed happy.

"Wake up, Dany," Frank said, nudging Dany's shoulder until he stirred. "Jean-Paul says they caught the saboteur and wants us to come downstairs as soon as we clean up."

"Why does he need us?" Dany muttered, pulling the covers back over his shoulder.

"He didn't say and I didn't ask," Frank replied. "He wants us there. That's all I needed to know."

Dany mumbled something else that Frank didn't catch, but he didn't ask. He suspected he didn't want to know. Instead, he nudged Dany one more time before going into the bathroom. His absence from bed would probably do more than anything else to wake Dany up. He was frequently amused by how much of a snuggler Dany was during the night. Frank liked to cuddle after sex. Dany liked to snuggle, period. Frank would regularly wake with a human blanket wrapped around him.

He showered quickly and came back into the room to find Dany digging in his suitcase for a fresh set of clothes. Grinning, he swatted Dany's bare backside playfully. Dany scowled at him, making Frank laugh. "Take a shower. Let's go see what's going on."

Dany disappeared into the bathroom, leaving Frank to dress in peace. He was curious to see what had happened during the night, but honestly it seemed almost unimportant. The sabotage on their car had put them behind in Portugal, but that had been balanced out by Ryan's poorer-than-usual showing in Italy, leaving them tied at the end of the seventh race. Since then, they'd run neck and neck in the overall standings, switching between first and second place depending on who won each rally. At the moment, Ryan was a few points ahead of them again, but Frank expected that to change after this race since the course in France was primarily asphalt, Dany's specialty. The home-field advantage was nothing to scoff at either, the fans having made their adoration of the Citroën team very clear over the days of preparation.

"Let's get this over with," Dany said, coming out of the bathroom, dressed but with his hair still wet. "I could use another few hours of sleep before the shakedown run this afternoon."

"Don't hold your breath," Frank said, shaking his head. "You know that isn't going to happen. We'll have to go to bed early tonight."

"We go to bed early every night," Dany said with an exaggerated leer. "We just don't go to sleep right away."

"You know what I meant," Frank retorted. "Come on. Jean-Paul's waiting."

They went down to the lobby of the hotel to find Jean-Paul, Isabelle, Ryan, and Ryan's head mechanic already waiting for them. "What's going on?" Dany asked.

"Our security guards caught someone trying to break into the garage during the night," Jean-Paul explained. "We don't know which car he intended to target, but it doesn't particularly matter. He was obviously up to no good. He's being questioned by the local police at the moment, but the race officials want to meet with us to see about pressing other charges besides breaking and entering."

"You'd better believe we'll press charges," Dany said. "Even though the damage only resulted in slower times in both cases, it might have had disastrous results. There isn't a whole lot of room for error on a rally course at the speeds we routinely drive."

"The problem is going to be proving he was responsible for the earlier incidents," Ryan said.

"That's not our problem," Dany insisted. "That's for the police to worry about. Our responsibility is to press charges so they can worry about it."

Ryan looked like he wasn't sure he agreed, but Isabelle's hand on his arm silenced any continued objections. Frank stifled his amusement once again at her influence on the hotheaded American.

"Do they know why he did it?" Frank asked.

"If they do, they haven't told me," Jean-Paul said. "We may learn more during the meeting with the race officials. Shall we go?"

They met with the rally officials at their headquarters in Strasbourg. Their faces were serious when everyone assembled finally. "Thank you all for joining us this morning. We have troubling news."

Frank took a seat at Dany's side, resisting the urge to reach for his lover's hand beneath the table as he waited for the officials to continue.

"The man we found isn't the one responsible for the damage?" Jean-Paul asked.

"That still remains to be determined, but it appears likely that he is," the official continued. "The troubling part is his identity."

"Another driver?" Ryan asked.

The official shook his head. "Another official. From what we have gathered so far, he appears to have operated under the misconception that he could help a fellow countryman move up in the standings by damaging your cars. We are still determining whether the driver was aware of the official's efforts on his 'behalf'. At the moment, it appears not so we will allow him to race today and not invalidate his results from the two rallies where the sabotage took place. If that changes, his results from those two races will be invalidated and he will be suspended for the rest of the season."

"Who is it?" Dany demanded.

"Until we know he was responsible, we aren't going to release that information," the official said. "If he isn't involved, we don't want his reputation damaged by an unfounded accusation."

It made sense, Frank decided, as the conversation continued around him. Anyone other than a race official would have been challenged coming to the parc ferme during the night, and while security had been tightened after the two sabotage attempts, the cars had still been locked up at night before that. Only an official would have had the key to get inside, and while the officials weren't necessarily mechanics of Isabelle's caliber, they had to have enough mechanical expertise to make sure the cars met WRC guidelines, certainly enough to disable the paddle shifter or to switch out a plug. He only hoped this was the end of it, other than figuring out if the other driver was involved as well, because he didn't want this tainting an otherwise extraordinary season.

THREE days later, having won the rally handily, Daniel rode a wave of euphoria into the hotel room before the obligatory celebration later that evening. Jean-Paul had given him a hard stare when he informed Daniel of the time the party started, but Daniel ignored him. He had plans that didn't involve anyone but himself, Frank, and their bed.

"I'm glad the officials cleared Garza of any involvement with the sabotage," Frank said as the door closed behind them. "Bad enough to have an official involved. It would have cast a pall over the whole sport to have a driver in on it as well."

Daniel murmured something noncommittal in reply, his focus firmly fixed on Frank. As far as he was concerned, the entire sabotage episode was behind them and good riddance.

"We should take quick showers," Frank went on, already tugging on his T-shirt. "We don't have all that long until the party starts."

Daniel bided his time, waiting until Frank had stripped to the waist before coming up behind his lover, arms going around Frank's waist to pull him tightly against Daniel's body. "They can start without us," he said, his voice gravelly with desire. "I have other plans for tonight."

"Oh really?" Frank asked, amusement coloring his voice.

"Really," Daniel said, rubbing his lengthening erection against Frank's ass. "And you're going to love every minute of it."

"Big words," Frank teased. "Are you sure you're up to following through?"

Daniel rutted against Frank's backside as he loosened his lover's pants and pushed them down, baring skin. "I'm sure."

Frank smirked over his shoulder, the expression spoiled by the groan that escaped him as Daniel's hand closed around his cock.

Daniel grinned back at him. "See?" he said. "I've already got you moaning. Give me another ten minutes and you'll be begging for me to fuck you."

"I don't beg," Frank replied immediately.

We'll see about that, Daniel thought with a grin, spinning Frank in his arms so their lengths rubbed together, the cloth of Daniel's pants adding an extra hint of friction on their skin. He spun them around, propelling Frank toward the bed rather than the bathroom. There would be time for showers later after they finished making love. For now, he wanted his lover beneath him, sweat, grime, and all.

Frank undulated beneath him as their lips met, ratcheting up the sensual tension and tempting Daniel to hurry the proceedings along. He made himself hold back, though. He didn't really care if Frank begged, but he wanted his lover so desperate by the time they joined that he would welcome Daniel inside him in exchange for his release.

"Why do you still have clothes on?" Frank asked between kisses, barely releasing Daniel's mouth long enough to speak. Daniel didn't try to answer, not wanting to give up the pleasure of Frank's lips for that long, but he did lift up enough to strip his pants and underwear off.

They both hissed into the kiss when Daniel settled back onto Frank's body, bare flesh rubbing together finally.

Frank shifted beneath Daniel as if to roll Daniel to his back, but Daniel shook his head, pinning Frank's hands. "Tonight *I* get to make love to *you*," he insisted. "Lie back and enjoy."

"I don't do passive very well," Frank said.

"You don't have to be passive," Daniel assured him. "You just can't take charge."

Frank looked like he wanted to protest again so Daniel kissed him, stopping the words before they could escape. As he did, he found one peaked nipple, rolling it between his fingers until Frank writhed beneath him, no longer seeking control. He kissed his way across to Frank's ear, nipping at the lobe before whispering, "Having you give in to me this way has to be the sexiest thing I've ever seen."

"I feel the same way every time you let me touch you," Frank gasped, turning his head to give Daniel better access to his neck. Daniel couldn't help himself. He fell on the long column of skin like a man starving, sucking and biting until Frank cried out with the joy of it. When Daniel lifted his head finally, he could see marks already starting to color the skin. The surge of possessive pride that swamped him at the sight felt ridiculously prehistoric, but he couldn't tamp down the smug grin on his face. Deciding he wanted to hear more of Frank's arousing gasps and moans, Daniel licked and nipped his way down Frank's chest to the hard bud he'd been teasing earlier. He could taste the sweat from the day as he sucked it into his mouth, but the saltiness only added to the eroticism of the moment, this huge, desperate need that couldn't be pigeonholed until after a shower or after the party. *Now*, it pounded in his blood. *Take him, claim him, love him now.*

Hand trembling with need, Daniel reached for the lube on the table next to the bed. He had no idea how long it had last been since Frank bottomed, but he knew it hadn't been recently, and the last thing he wanted was to cause his lover any pain. Frank hissed softly when the cool gel-coated fingers danced across his entrance, but he made no move to pull away. Daniel teased more deliberately, needing more of a sign than lack of rejection that Frank wanted this.

The way Frank's legs drifted slowly apart, as if he still wasn't quite sure he was ready and yet wanted it anyway, turned Daniel inside out. He pressed one slick finger into Frank as he lowered his head to mouth Frank's cock. The mewl that escaped his lover nearly stole his control, but he fought down the urge to rush, to ram into Frank and never come out again.

Frank's guardian muscle spasmed around Daniel's finger, making him long to feel that sensation around his cock. He worked the digit deeper, massaging the outer ring with his thumb as the tip of his finger found Frank's prostate, playing across it repeatedly. He didn't need the shout above him to let him know he'd hit it. The sudden burst of fluid across his tongue told him all he needed to know.

When the constriction around his finger eased somewhat, he added a second one, twisting and scissoring them to stretch Frank for the larger girth of his cock. He wasn't a size queen, but he wasn't a small man, either, and he didn't want this to be a one-time event.

Eventually Frank's guardian muscle relaxed enough that Daniel lifted his head from his feasting. "Are you ready or do you want another finger?"

"Fuck me already," Frank pleaded. Daniel hid a grin as he reached for the condom. He wasn't entirely sure that counted as begging, but it was close enough. Frank wanted him, wanted *this*, and nothing else mattered. He rolled the latex sheath over his erection and coated it quickly with lube, ignoring Frank's impatient mutterings.

Daniel lined himself up, rocking persistently against Frank's entrance until the muscle relaxed and let him in. Even with the condom, the heat of Frank's body stole Daniel's breath. He could only imagine what it feel like with nothing between them, but that was a thought and a discussion for another time. For now, he concentrated on working his way deeper into Frank, leaning forward so their mouths met, tongues twining together in the other half of the mating ritual.

Frank pushed up against him, his hands closing over Daniel's ass to urge him on. Daniel didn't need any more encouragement than that, taking his rhythm from Frank's movements until every thrust went deep and every withdrawal nearly separated them. Never completely, though. Nothing would separate them completely if Daniel had any say in the matter. He'd found the partner of his dreams: someone who loved racing as much as he did and yet loved him even more. Daniel intended to spend the rest of his life making sure Frank knew how much he was loved.

Starting right now.

"I love you," he murmured, breaking their kiss momentarily.

"I love you too," Frank said, his hands clenching harder on Daniel's ass. "Now stop talking and make me come!"

Daniel chuckled, his hips moving faster in response to his lover's order. Even when he bottomed, Frank would never be submissive. Daniel could live with that. He had enough responsibility when he was driving. It would feel good to let someone else take control away from the race course. Sometimes, anyway.

Shifting enough that he could work a hand between their bodies, he encircled Frank's cock, stroking it in time with his thrusts.

Frank thrashed beneath him, his hips lifting jerkily into Daniel's hand, throwing off the rhythm, but it hardly mattered as Frank's release hit him, his ass clenching around Daniel's erection as he coated their chests with creamy fluid. The expression on his face sent Daniel over the edge as well, his hips stuttering against Frank's as he collapsed forward onto his lover. "So beautiful," he murmured against Frank's neck. "The most beautiful thing I've ever seen."

"I love you too," Frank said, and this time his voice was rich with satiation and contentment rather than with impatience. Daniel smiled. He could live with that too.

EPILOGUE

DANIEL and Frank waited behind two other drivers to take the podium in Wales at the end of the final rally of the season. Daniel couldn't decide if Ryan's absence from the line in front of him made his victory sweeter or not. When the season began, he would have crowed over the accident that forced Ryan to retire from the race after the fourth stage, the other driver having pushed a bend at high speed in his bid to win the final rally, but things had changed over the course of the year. Glancing at the man sitting beside him, he knew what had changed the most. Win or lose this rally, this season, this year or next, Daniel had the ultimate prize in his co-driver's seat.

"You ready for this?" he asked.

"Ready for the season to be over?" Frank teased. "Yeah, I'm looking forward to a break."

That wasn't what Daniel meant, but he let it go. He and Frank had discussed their plan for the afternoon as soon as they realized what their win would mean.

The car ahead of him pulled off the podium, and the race organizers gestured for him to take his place as the winner of the rally. He gunned the engine and drove up onto the grandstand, stopping next to the emcee. He stepped out, Frank mimicking him on the opposite side of the car and coming around to stand at Daniel's side as he had at every rally they'd won. Daniel doubted anyone else thought anything about it, but it was one of those little gestures that Daniel considered so important.

The emcee arrived at their side, shaking hands with both of them. "Congratulations! This is a big win for you today. Not only the Rally Wales, but the championship."

"It is quite a thrill," Daniel agreed, his heart pounding with excitement and nerves. "It has been a challenging season."

"Exciting is the word for it from our perspective," the emcee agreed. "No clear winner until the last rally of the season. It's been quite a few years since we've had it come down to the wire this way."

"We were sorry to see Michaels out of the race yesterday and today," Frank said. Daniel shot him a grateful smile. They had discussed what to say if Ryan came up in the interview, but Daniel knew he wouldn't be able to manage the English on his own. They were partners now, so it didn't matter which of them answered the questions, not in his mind. "He's a valiant competitor and a good friend, and it would have been an honor to share the podium with him today."

"Ah, but if you were sharing the podium with him, you might not be taking home the championship trophy," the emcee reminded him.

"Then I'd be cheering for him along with everyone else," Daniel said firmly. "If he had outraced us here in Wales, he would have deserved the trophy."

"So what are your plans for the off months?" the emcee asked.

"We'll go back to Clermont-Ferrand as always," Daniel said. "My sister is already talking about tweaks she wants to make on the car before next season starts, and if she changes things, then we have to learn the new systems."

"It sounds like it will be a busy winter for you, then," the emcee said.

"Yes, as always."

"What about you, Frank?" the emcee asked. "Will you go back to France as well or are you headed for Canada?"

"We're definitely going back to France first," Frank replied, the deliberate use of the plural pronoun making Daniel smile. "We'll have to see what Isabelle has in store for us and the timeline for it before we can make plans beyond that."

"Well, I wish you both the best of luck," the emcee said, shaking their hands again. "And here are the rally organizers with the champagne."

Daniel took one bottle, waiting for Frank to take the other one and circle to his side of the car before climbing onto the roof. They shook the bottles as the team rushed from the sidelines to circle the car, cheering loudly as they came. Daniel caught sight of Ryan in the crowd, Isabelle leaving his side as she joined the rest of the crew. "Je t'aime," Daniel murmured softly as he shook the bottle of champagne.

"Je t'aime aussi," Frank whispered back.

When the team had gathered around the car, Daniel popped the cork on his bottle, spraying the car and the team with champagne. Frank followed suit barely a second behind. As the champagne fountained around them, Daniel turned to face Frank, reaching for his lover's hand. Frank's fingers curled around his in silent encouragement and eager possession.

Daniel smiled, leaning in to press his lips to Frank's.

The cheers of the team surrounding them only got louder.

Daniel lingered for a moment but not overly long. "Think they got the idea?"

Frank grinned. "Kiss me again, just in case they missed it the first time."

ARIEL TACHNA lives in southwestern Ohio with her husband, her daughter and son, and their cat. A native of the region, she has nonetheless lived all over the world, having fallen in love with both France, where she found her career and her husband, and India, where she dreams of retiring some day. She started writing when she was twelve and hasn't looked back since. A connoisseur of wine and horses, she's as comfortable on a farm as she is in the big cities of the world.

Visit Ariel's web site at http://www.arieltachna.com/ and her blog at http://arieltachna.livejournal.com/.

Contemporary Romance by ARIEL TACHNA

http://www.dreamspinnerpress.com

Also by ARIEL TACHNA

Historical Romance by ARIEL TACHNA

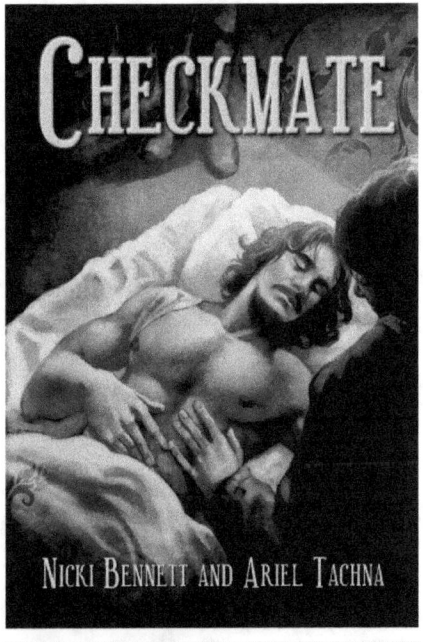

www.ingramcontent.com/pod-product-compliance
Lightning Source LLC
Chambersburg PA
CBHW070703280626
47159CB00022B/1805